The Class Trip

Elizabeth looked around at the lush green lawn bordered with a rainbow of pink, red, white, and yellow flowers. Everything sparkled with color.

"Hurry up, you guys," Julie called. "Maybe we can get a seat on the steam locomotive."

They walked through the glass tunnel that led into the park, glancing up at the artificial waterfall that cascaded all around them.

Elizabeth drew in her breath as they emerged from the short tunnel. It was like entering another world.

Right in front of them was the main depot for the old-fashioned steam locomotive that wound its way around the park. To the left was a shrub-bordered path that led to the Fun Zone, the section that contained the roller coaster, the bumper cars, and other conventional rides. To the right was Fairy Tale Land, where the rides and attractions had fantasy themes. That was Elizabeth's favorite part of the park.

She took another deep breath. Everything here was so magical. It seemed as if anything could happen today.

Bantam Skylark Books in the SWEET VALLEY TWINS series
Ask your bookseller for the books you have missed

#1 BEST FRIENDS
#2 TEACHER'S PET
#3 THE HAUNTED HOUSE
#4 CHOOSING SIDES
#5 SNEAKING OUT
#6 THE NEW GIRL
#7 THREE'S A CROWD
#8 FIRST PLACE
#9 AGAINST THE RULES
#10 ONE OF THE GANG
#11 BURIED TREASURE
#12 KEEPING SECRETS
#13 STRETCHING THE TRUTH
#14 TUG OF WAR
#15 THE OLDER BOY
#16 SECOND BEST
#17 BOYS AGAINST GIRLS
#18 CENTER OF ATTENTION

Sweet Valley Twins Super Edition

#1 THE CLASS TRIP

SWEET VALLEY TWINS
◇ SUPER EDITION ◇

The Class Trip

Written by
Jamie Suzanne

Created by
FRANCINE PASCAL

A BANTAM SKYLARK BOOK®
TORONTO · NEW YORK · LONDON · SYDNEY · AUCKLAND

THE CLASS TRIP

A Bantam Skylark Book / June 1988

*Sweet Valley High® and Sweet Valley Twins are
trademarks of Francine Pascal.*

Conceived by Francine Pascal

Cover art by James Mathewuse.

*Produced by Daniel Weiss Associates, Inc.
27 West 20 Street
New York, NY 10011*

*Skylark Books is a registered trademark of Bantam Books.
Registered in U.S. Patent and Trademark Office and elsewhere.*

ISBN 0-553-15588-1

Published simultaneously in the United States and Canada

*Bantam Books are published by Bantam Books, a division of Bantam
Doubleday Dell Publishing Group, Inc. Its trademark, consisting of the
words "Bantam Books" and the portrayal of a rooster, is Registered in
U.S. Patent and Trademark Office and in other countries. Marca Regis-
trada. Bantam Books, 666 Fifth Avenue, New York, New York 10103.*

PRINTED IN THE UNITED STATES OF AMERICA

O   0 9 8 7 6 5 4 3 2 1

With special thanks
for all their help—
Rebecca Quaretti-Lee
and Billy Carmen

One

◇

"Elizabeth!" Jessica Wakefield practically shouted as she skipped through the bathroom linking her bedroom with her twin sister's room and sat down hard on the bed. "Lizzie," she pleaded, "wake up!"

"What? What is it, Jess? Is something wrong?" The blond head that appeared from beneath the crumpled sheets was a mirror image of Jessica's. Both girls had long, sun-streaked blond hair, blue-green eyes, and dimples in their left cheeks.

Elizabeth frowned at her sister. "Why are you up so early?"

"Don't you remember what day it is, silly?" Jessica asked.

"Of course! The class trip!" Suddenly as excited as her sister, Elizabeth forgot all about her interrupted sleep. She jumped out of bed and reached for her blue robe.

"I'm so excited. A whole school day at the Enchanted Forest! I didn't think today would ever come," Jessica said.

Elizabeth smiled at her sister as she slipped her arms into the sleeves of her bathrobe. Only something very special could have gotten Jessica out of bed so early. Elizabeth was usually the first one up and most of the time she had to coax Jessica out of bed to make sure they got to school on time. But today was different. The entire sixth grade would be spending the day at one of the biggest amusement parks on the West Coast.

"What are you going to wear?" Jessica asked Elizabeth.

"My white jeans and blue top," Elizabeth answered quickly. "What about you?"

Jessica gave the question some thought. "Maybe my lavender slacks and striped blouse. Or maybe my green jumpsuit would look better. Then there's my new pink and white outfit—"

Elizabeth grinned as she made her bed, then headed for the bathroom. "Better make up your mind, Jess. I smell bacon and eggs. You wouldn't want to miss breakfast, would you?"

Jessica ignored her sister's warning and headed

toward the phone in the hall. "I'm going to call Lila to see what she's wearing." Lila Fowler was one of Jessica's best friends and, like Jessica, was a member of the Unicorn Club, a group of popular girls who considered themselves as special as the mythical animal for which the club was named.

Elizabeth thought the club was silly. As far as she could tell, the members spent all their time talking about clothes and gossiping about boys.

As usual, Elizabeth was dressed and ready long before Jessica came skipping down the stairs to the sunny Spanish-tiled kitchen. Jessica had decided to wear her green jumpsuit, but her blond hair was still uncombed.

Mrs. Wakefield was lifting a fluffy omelet from a hot skillet. She smiled at her daughters. "You two look awfully eager to get to school this morning."

"They sure do." Steven, their fourteen-year-old brother, sat at the kitchen table wolfing down a plateful of bacon and eggs. "Too bad the sixth grade doesn't go to the Enchanted Forest every day. Then Jessica would always be on time."

Everyone smiled but Jessica. Her aversion to early rising was a family joke. She made a face at her brother and said, "Just because you like to get to school early to play basketball doesn't mean everyone should get up at dawn!"

Steven was a dedicated basketball player who practiced year-round. He grinned at Jessica's taunt and said, "That's what makes me so good."

"A sports whiz, and modest, too!" Jessica said with a giggle. "It's amazing that someone who eats as much as you can even move around the court."

"Yeah," Elizabeth said, eyeing an empty plate on the table. "Did you polish off all the bacon already?"

"No fair," Jessica chimed in. "Mom!"

"Don't worry, girls. There's plenty more in the oven." Accustomed to her son's healthy appetite, Mrs. Wakefield had already prepared more bacon. She set it on the table and divided the omelet between the twins. "Eat up. You have a long bus ride to the Forest this morning."

Jessica and Elizabeth began chattering nonstop about the day's plans—what they would eat, all the rides they'd go on, what new rides that had opened since their last visit.

It wasn't until Elizabeth carried her empty plate and glass to the sink that she remembered she had something important to discuss with Jessica.

"You haven't forgotten what you promised me yesterday, have you, Jess?" she asked.

When Jessica didn't answer, Elizabeth spun around, ready to plead with her twin to keep the promise she had made. But her sister had already slipped out of the kitchen. Elizabeth sighed loudly as she rinsed her plate and put it in the dishwasher.

"Is something wrong, dear?" Mrs. Wakefield asked.

Elizabeth hesitated. "It's no big deal. Yesterday Caroline Pearce asked me if I would sit with her on the bus today."

Mrs. Wakefield nodded. "And . . . that's not good?"

Elizabeth shook her head. "Caroline's the biggest gossip at school, Mom. I hate the thought of having to ride all the way to the Enchanted Forest beside her! If I had to listen to all her stories, I'd have gray hair before we got there."

Mrs. Wakefield laughed. "I don't think so, Elizabeth. So did you tell her no?"

"I didn't want to hurt her feelings," Elizabeth explained. "And I hadn't made plans to sit with anyone else."

"So you told Caroline you'd sit with her," Mrs.

Wakefield said. "What does this have to do with Jessica?"

Elizabeth took a big swallow. "Well, I didn't exactly say yes to Caroline. I sort of made up a story. I told Caroline I had promised to sit with Jessica. Then I told Jessica I really needed her to sit with me because of the story I'd told Caroline. Jessica promised me she would."

"So what's the problem?" Mrs. Wakefield asked. "Sounds as if everything's fine to me."

But Elizabeth wasn't as sure as her mother. She knew that Jessica forgot promises as easily as she made them. "No problem yet. I just hope Jessica hasn't forgotten."

Just then Jessica reappeared in the doorway, her long hair carefully arranged in soft waves around her face. "Come on, Lizzie. Let's go. 'Bye, Mom." Without waiting for her twin, she hurried out the door.

Elizabeth went running after her.

Elizabeth meant to remind Jessica of her promise on the way to school but she never had the chance. Jessica chattered on and on without letting Elizabeth get a word in.

"I can't wait to go on that gigantic new roller

coaster," Jessica said. "Ken Matthews said he heard one car even goes backward!"

Elizabeth frowned. She'd heard that the brand new Super Coaster was ten stories tall, higher than any building in Sweet Valley, and that the cars moved at over one hundred miles an hour. Never a big fan of roller coasters, she was in no hurry to try this one.

"Oh, Lizzie," Jessica squealed. "This is going to be so much fun! We're going to have the time of our lives."

Jessica walked so fast that Elizabeth had to practically run to keep up with her. They reached the school grounds in record time and hurried toward the big yellow bus parked in front. Although they were a little early, most of the other sixth-graders were already there and boarding the bus.

"Hurry, Jess. There aren't many seats left." Elizabeth climbed in and searched for an empty seat. She spotted her best friend, Amy Sutton, sharing a seat with Julie Porter. "Since you're sitting with Jessica, I asked Julie to sit with me," Amy explained. "Aren't you excited? I could hardly eat my breakfast! I got here a half-hour ago."

"We've been waiting forever for this trip," Julie added.

"I know," Elizabeth said. "My stomach's all in knots. Well, I'd better hurry and find a seat," she said to her two friends. "I hate sitting all the way in the back; I get carsick back there."

She hurried on toward one of the few empty seats near the front, then turned to wave at her twin.

"Hurry up, Jess."

Elizabeth sat down and waited impatiently for her sister. All around her, her classmates chattered and laughed. At the front of the bus, Mr. Bowman, one of Elizabeth's favorite teachers, clasped a clipboard and checked the names of the arriving sixth-graders off a list. He and Ms. Wyler were chaperoning the trip, and Elizabeth giggled when she saw them trying to count the number of students already on the bus.

"Settle down and stay in your seats," Mr. Bowman said. "I don't want to miss anyone."

When Jessica didn't join her right away, Elizabeth began to worry. She didn't want to get up because she might lose her seat. If only she had brought along something to mark her seat with. The only thing she had was her small flash camera, and she wasn't about to let that out of her sight.

"Jessica!" Elizabeth called.

Her sister still didn't answer, so Elizabeth finally stood up and walked toward the front of the bus. To her chagrin, she discovered Jessica sitting beside Lila Fowler.

Elizabeth frowned. "Jessica?"

"Hi, Lizzie. Did you find a good seat yet?"

"You're supposed to be sitting with me, remember?" Elizabeth's voice shook as she tried to contain her anger.

"But I promised Lila I'd sit with her, Lizzie," Jessica said, smiling sweetly. "And she saved me this seat."

"But you promised *me*, Jessie!"

"I asked first," Lila said. "Don't be such a baby, Elizabeth. I asked Jessica to sit with me this morning when she called to see what I was wearing."

Elizabeth, looking from Lila's violet jumpsuit to Jessica's green one, felt her anger grow. "But I asked you yesterday, Jessica."

Jessica looked only slightly guilty. "I really forgot. When Lila asked me this morning, I said yes. And by the time I remembered, I'd said yes to you, too, I'd already hung up. And now, after Lila saved me a seat and we dressed alike and all, how could I possibly say no? Don't be angry, Lizzie. You have lots of friends on the bus."

Elizabeth gritted her teeth. "Sure, but everyone else already has someone to sit with!"

She looked around. Amy sat beside Julie, Nora Mercandy sat with Brooke Dennis, and even the seat Elizabeth had first selected had been filled by Randy Mason and Winston Egbert. The only seat left was all the way at the back of the bus.

Elizabeth groaned.

"Elizabeth," someone called. "You can still sit with me."

Elizabeth knew that voice. It belonged to the one person she had wanted to avoid—Caroline Pearce.

"Thank you, Caroline," Elizabeth said with a sigh, sitting down reluctantly.

Mr. Bowman finished checking his list and nodded to the bus driver. "OK. I think we're ready." The English teacher sat down beside Ms. Wyler as the big bus began to roll forward.

"We're off!" Jerry McAllister yelled, leading a round of cheers.

Elizabeth was the only one who remained quiet.

Beside her, Caroline said, "Wait till you hear what I heard yesterday from Kimberly Haver about Bruce Patman's crush on a high school cheerleader."

Elizabeth tried not to grimace. It was going to be a very long ride. *I'm never going to forgive Jessica,* she thought as she settled back in her seat.

Two

◇

Elizabeth's mood began to lighten as the bus headed up the winding road that led to the Enchanted Forest. Finally she spotted the entrance and let out a sigh of relief. The rest of the class erupted in a loud cheer.

"We're here!" Amy yelled.

"I'm going straight to the water slide," Jerry McAllister announced. "It's my all-time favorite."

"But it's too early to get wet," Charlie Cashman argued. "Let's go to the Moonwalk first."

"What about the Mirror Maze?" Lila asked. "That's got to be the best!"

Everyone on the bus talked at once as they drove through the gates to the parking lot. Once the bus was still, Mr. Bowman held up a hand for silence, waiting patiently for the excited sixth-graders to quiet down.

"Ms. Wyler and I are going to pay for your admission," he announced. "I want all of you to wait in one line until we're ready to go in. Then you may split up and go wherever you like. I'm sure you all want to do different things."

Shouts of approval rose from the excited group.

"Listen up, everyone. We'll meet at the clock tower near the front entrance at six o'clock sharp. It's up to you. If you're not there at six, you'll have a long walk home."

He paused and looked around. "Now where are we going to meet?"

"The clock tower!" the students chorused.

"Good." Mr. Bowman nodded. "If anyone stubs a toe or gets a stomachache, go to the first-aid station and have me paged. Any questions?"

"When can we start?" Charlie shouted.

Mr. Bowman laughed. "Line up outside the bus. As class president, Randy can be first. OK, Randy? I'm counting on you to keep the rest of the class in order. All right. I'm off to get the tickets."

Randy Mason grinned at this honor and jumped off the bus. As the rest of the sixth-graders scrambled to follow him, Elizabeth breathed another sigh of relief. She was released from Caroline's company, at last.

"Thanks for letting me sit with you, Caroline," she said politely.

"Sure. See you later," Caroline said as she made her way to the front of the bus.

"Right." Elizabeth sighed again. Well, at least she didn't have to spend the entire day with her.

She stepped off the bus and got in line with Amy and Julie.

"What do you guys want to do first?" Amy asked.

"How about the Ferris wheel?" Julie suggested.

"I love the bumper cars. But maybe we should try a new ride first." Amy jumped up and down, unable to make up her mind.

"I want to try them all," Elizabeth said. "But first, I want to go on my very favorite ride—King Abelard's Castle."

"Yeah, that's one of the best," Amy agreed. "Good idea, Elizabeth. Let's go there first."

The girls waited impatiently for their teachers to return with the tickets.

"This is great," Amy said. "The park just opened, so it won't be very crowded yet."

"I can tell this is going to be a perfect day," Elizabeth said. But then she caught sight of Jessica and Lila. Arms linked, heads close, they seemed to be plotting their day's schedule. The sight of them reminded Elizabeth of her sister's betrayal, and she frowned.

"What's the matter, Elizabeth?" Amy asked. "You look upset all of a sudden."

"Nothing," Elizabeth answered quickly. Seeing Amy's hurt look, she tried to soften her abrupt reply. "I mean, I'm fine, really. We're going to have a great time today, and nothing is going to bother us."

The line suddenly surged forward, and Elizabeth and her friends swept through the turnstile, giving their tickets to a smiling attendant.

Elizabeth looked around at the lush green lawn bordered with a rainbow of pink, red, white, and yellow flowers. Everything sparkled with color.

"Hurry up, you guys," Julie called. "Maybe we can get a seat on the steam locomotive."

They walked through the glass tunnel that led into the park, glancing up at the artificial waterfall that cascaded all around them.

Elizabeth drew in her breath as they emerged from the short tunnel. It was like entering another world.

Right in front of them was the main depot for the old-fashioned steam locomotive that wound its way around the park. To the left was a shrub-bordered path that led to the Fun Zone, the section that contained the roller coaster, the bumper cars, and other conventional rides. To the right was Fairy Tale Land, where the rides and attractions had fantasy themes. That was Elizabeth's favorite part of the park.

She took another deep breath. Everything here was so magical. It seemed as if anything could happen today. "Let's go," she yelled. Julie and Amy ran after her toward the train stop.

They waited only a minute or two before a large black and red locomotive pulled into view. The driver, in his blue overalls, cap, and red bandanna, grinned at the girls as they clambered on board the open-air car behind him. Elizabeth took a front seat, and Amy and Julie sat down beside her. Elizabeth leaned over the edge of her bright yellow seat and waved at her classmates still on the street.

"Elizabeth! Let's meet at Little Red Riding Hood's House for lunch," someone yelled.

Elizabeth looked down and groaned. It was Caroline. "Sorry, I've made plans already," she called back, relieved that Amy and Julie were with her.

The engineer blew his whistle, and the train moved slowly down the street. Elizabeth bounced up and down in her seat with excitement.

But then she thought of Jessica and Lila and her good mood faded. No matter how hard she tried, it seemed she couldn't forget Jessica's broken promise.

Lila and Jessica stopped to admire a window display of tiny crystal animals in one of the shops just inside the entrance.

"I want to go to the Mirror Maze first," Lila said, her tone commanding.

"Why don't we take a ride on the Super Coaster on the way?" Jessica suggested.

"No." Lila shook her head. "I want to go straight to the mirrors."

"But we're going right past the roller coaster," Jessica argued.

"So what? We've got all day here." Lila snapped.

"Yes, but—" Jessica paused to consult her map of the park so she could convince Lila she had a better plan. When she looked up again, Lila was gone!

"Lila?" Jessica looked around and spotted her friend in front of the next shop, talking to a tall, incredibly cute boy with wavy blond hair and deep blue eyes.

"Wow," Jessica murmured, irritated that Lila had seen him first. It didn't help that the boy was grinning at an adoring Lila. Jessica edged closer to the pair, determined to give the stranger a chance to notice her, too.

"Hi," she said brightly. Giving Lila a nudge, she waited for an introduction.

Lila hesitated just a moment. "Jessica, this is Alex Bellford, from northern California. We met at camp last summer. Although"—she batted her eyes slightly toward the tall boy—"I almost didn't recognize him. He's grown at least two inches since then."

And he's pretty cute, too, Jessica thought. She smiled at Alex, who grinned back. "Nice to meet you. Are you here on a school trip, too?"

"No," Alex said. "I'm here on my own. My dad had to come to Los Angeles on a short business trip and brought me along. I'm spending the day here while he attends his meetings."

Lila didn't seem terribly pleased at the way Alex grinned at her friend. "Alex and I are going to ride the Haunted Tunnel," she told Jessica. "I know you wanted to go to the roller coaster first, so how about if I meet you in an hour or so at Hansel and Gretel's Woods?"

Jessica watched openmouthed as Lila and Alex walked off together without even waiting for her answer.

Some friend she is, Jessica fumed to herself. *We were supposed to spend the day together.*

She frowned after Lila for a moment. Then, determined not to let Lila spoil her time, she debated whether to check out the shops or head for the rides.

Noticing a group of her classmates just ahead of her, she ran to meet them.

"Hey, Ellen," Jessica called. "Wait for me."

Elizabeth, Amy, and Julie rode the train into Fairy Tale Land, gazing at the sights around them. The Enchanted Forest was built on a bluff overlooking the Pacific and the ocean sparkled under the cloudless blue sky. The bright sun reflected off the rides, too, and made the park look as if it really was straight out of a book of fairy tales. Elizabeth's heart fluttered with delight. She was determined to forget about Jessica and enjoy herself today.

Amy nudged her as they passed the Ape Man's Safari ride. "Look down there," she cried. "There's the Farmer In the Dell."

Elizabeth turned back toward the main plaza

and stared at the life-size characters who acted out the nursery song every fifteen minutes. It had been her favorite attraction when she was little. She felt a little funny now, realizing it wasn't even on her list of things to see today. "I hope we catch up with Prince Valiant," she said. "I'd like to get my picture taken with him."

"I'll be on the lookout," Julie said.

The train stopped at a plaza that led to several rides. The three girls jumped down to the pavement and walked in the direction of King Abelard's Castle.

"Oh, let's take Ali Baba's Treasure Hunt next," Julie begged, pointing to the entrance to that ride.

"Then we can walk through Dracula's Haunted House," Amy suggested. "I *love* getting scared, and that place really gives me the creeps."

"OK," Elizabeth said. "But first, the king's castle."

She led the way toward the huge gray stone building. Tall, wispy-leaved eucalyptus trees surrounded the castle, giving it an eerie and magical look. A moat separated the castle from the rest of the park, and a few moments later the girls got on line for the boat ride that would take them there.

"Hey, Lizzie, wait up."

Elizabeth froze at the sound of Jessica's voice.

"Elizabeth," Julie said. "Jessica's calling. Didn't you hear her?"

Elizabeth did hear her, but she was pretending she didn't. She took her place in line without so much as a backward glance. *It's about time Jessica had a dose of her own medicine. I'm not going to forgive her so quickly this time.* She simply had to learn not to treat other people so thoughtlessly.

When the girls got to the front of the line, the ride attendant motioned them to a red boat. Elizabeth and Amy climbed into the front seat and sat down. The rest of the seats filled up quickly, and with a sudden lurch, the boat began to move. They were off to visit the fantasy land of royalty and knights in shining armor.

Right after they left the dock, Elizabeth turned to see where Jessica was sitting. A twinge of guilt made her stomach do a flip.

Poor Jessica sat all alone in the very last seat.

Three

◇

Elizabeth tried not to think of her sister as the boat glided across the inky black water. She stared at the castle and imagined for a minute what it would have been like to live in the Middle Ages. Would she have been a member of the king's court—or a lowly serf?

Her thoughts were interrupted by Amy's scream. "Elizabeth, look over there!"

Creeping out from behind one of the many rocks in the moat was an ugly green alligator. He snapped his giant teeth at the crowded boat.

"It's only a fake," Elizabeth told Amy.

"I know." Her friend was breathing easier now. "But it sure looks real."

The boat maneuvered around another rock and glided into the dark castle. To the right was the grand center courtyard which was filled with members of the king's court. A magician stood in one corner waving his wand over a kettle of magical brew. Ladies in high-pointed hats curtsied to each other as a court jester did flips while juggling flaming sticks in the air.

In the next room, the mythical King Abelard stood at the head of an enormous table with a huge goblet in his hand. A roast pig's head with an apple in its mouth rested on the table in front of him. The queen, dressed regally in a shimmering white gown, sat beside him. Trumpets blared as the sounds of merriment echoed through the dark passages.

Then, suddenly, a particularly grotesque-looking guest leaned out over the water, practically touching their boat, and called, "Come join the party."

Amy jumped. "Oooh, he scared me."

Elizabeth nodded. He *was* scary-looking. She drew a deep breath as the boat slipped deeper into the castle. Strange animal noises bellowed in the darkness, and Elizabeth shivered when a black cat suddenly came into view. It looked as if it were about to jump into the boat, but it was snatched away by an evil-looking wizard just in time. Elizabeth reached out to touch Amy's arm. She was glad to have her friend beside her.

Both girls jumped suddenly when a gargoyle on

the wall above them began to speak. Shrieking, they clutched at each other as the boat dipped sharply beneath them. Elizabeth felt her stomach flip-flop and swallowed hard.

Against the wall on the left, Elizabeth caught sight of two knights engaged in a sword fight. An empty suit of armor was in the next room, a skeleton lying alongside it.

Then the boat made a sharp turn and left the castle, crossing the moat out into the sunlight again. Right before them was a grassy field, and as the boat drew closer, Elizabeth saw two knights on horseback on either side of the moat. Clutching huge lances in their armored hands, the knights began to charge toward each other.

"They're going to hit us!" Amy shrieked.

Elizabeth laughed nervously. "Amy, it's only a ride," she said. But she grabbed her friend's arm and held on tightly.

The knights clashed just as the boat sailed into a tunnel below them.

"It seems so real," Elizabeth said with a gulp. She was surprised how much the ride scared her, even though she'd been on it several times before. Then she remembered Jessica, sitting all alone at the back of the boat. If she were this scared sitting with

Amy, Elizabeth thought, she could just imagine how Jessica felt. Then she pushed all thoughts of her twin aside as the boat made another sharp turn back into the dark castle.

They rode past a small room in one of the castle's towers. Inside was a young blond-haired girl who gripped the iron bars that separated her from the boat. "Help me," she called, "please help me get out of here."

The girl reminded Elizabeth of Jessica.

But she pushed thoughts of her sister out of her mind again as the boat veered downward through a series of catacombs. Thin, hollow-eyed men peered out from behind the pillars, chains on their legs. Fierce-looking guards held medieval maces and daggers. Every now and then a skeleton popped into the girls' vision. Moans from the cavernous pit brought goose bumps to Elizabeth's arms.

She thought of Jessica again, a whisper of guilt accompanying her thoughts. *I shouldn't have ignored her. I should have made up with her when I had the chance.* '

Then Amy cried, "Liz, look out!"

Elizabeth glanced up to where Amy was pointing. A huge double-headed ax swung back and forth, suspended over the boat right over their heads! "Oh, no!" she shrieked. "It's going to chop our heads off!" Gasping, she looked back to check on Jessica.

Amy moved just as Elizabeth turned and their heads knocked together with numbing force.

"Ow!" Elizabeth cried.

"Ouch! My head," Amy moaned.

For a moment Elizabeth felt stunned as images blurred before her eyes. Then she blinked, the boat steadied beneath her, and everything went back into place.

"Wow. We really hit hard," Amy said, rubbing her forehead. "I'm going to be black and blue."

"Me, too," Elizabeth said. "Are you OK?"

"Fine," Amy answered. "That was a close call. I really did think the ax would get us."

"I know. Me, too," Elizabeth said as the boat slid back out into the daylight. When they reached the dock, she stretched her arms up over her head and got ready to disembark.

"That was great," Julie said from behind them, jumping out of her seat.

Listening to Amy and Julie giggle, Elizabeth began to feel guilty again. *I'm going to be miserable all day unless I fix things up with Jessica,* she thought. So she decided to make up with her twin and forget about the broken promise.

But when Elizabeth turned toward the back of the boat, the last seat was empty and the path behind the boat was deserted.

"Jessica must have jumped out awfully quickly," she said to Amy in surprise.

"I don't blame her for being in such a hurry," Amy said. "There's so much to see. Come on. Let's go."

"She probably ran so she wouldn't have to see me," Elizabeth said. "I wouldn't speak to her before the ride. I'm sure she's mad at me."

She frowned. Even though her twin often gave her reason to be angry, Elizabeth never felt quite right until things were straightened out between them.

But there was nothing she could do about it now. Jessica was nowhere in sight.

"Hey, the new Caterpillar Cavern is right over here. Let's try it," Julie was saying to the girls.

"That sounds great," Amy said.

"Wait. I want to find Jessica first," Elizabeth told her friends.

"She's probably already at the Caterpillar ride,"

Amy insisted. "So you might as well come with us and talk to her there."

That seemed reasonable, so Elizabeth followed her friends to the ride. She looked for Jessica when they got in line, but two tall kids blocked her view.

In a few minutes they approached the entrance to the cavern. Elizabeth sat down in the middle of a caterpillar-shaped train that would take them through a multi-leveled underground chamber.

The ride started with a lurch. They slunk down a steep ramp to a large, subterranean cavern. Lizards, mice, and moles flashed into the girls' line of vision, and it looked as though they might jump straight into the train with them. But Elizabeth wasn't enjoying the experience one bit. Looking over the crowded, twisting train, she saw no trace of her sister.

When they rounded a corner and came face to face with a larger-than-life caterpillar, Elizabeth forgot about Jessica for a moment and grabbed Amy's arm.

When the ride ended, the two girls climbed out of the caterpillar train, gasping with relief. As they walked out into the bright sunshine, Amy said, "That was great! Where do you want to go next?"

Elizabeth, determined not to do another thing

until she found Jessica, said, "You guys go on ahead if you want, but I've got to find my sister."

The amusement park was beginning to fill up, and Elizabeth knew it was going to be more difficult to find Jessica in the crowd.

"Look," Amy said. "There're some kids from Sweet Valley. Maybe they'll know where Jessica is."

Elizabeth waved at the group and hurried to catch up. "Have you seen Jessica?" she asked Charlie Cashman. He had just gotten off the Moonwalk and he looked a little dizzy.

"I haven't seen her since we got off the bus," he told Elizabeth.

But Jerry McAllister said, "I think I saw her and Lila heading for Blind Man's Bluff. That's where we're going next. Want to come?"

Elizabeth nodded and fell into step. But when the two boys stopped to buy a bag of popcorn, Elizabeth hurried on ahead of them, eager to catch up with her sister.

Elizabeth saw Lila and a boy she didn't know coming out of Blind Man's Bluff. "Have you seen Jessica?" she asked.

Lila shook her head. "Not for a while. Maybe she went to the Super Coaster."

"Good. I'm going to head over there now."

"You'd better hurry," Lila told her. "It's easy to get lost in a big place like this."

"I know. That's why I've got to find her now," Elizabeth insisted.

"I'm going to stay and get on this ride," Amy said. "You don't mind, do you?"

"I'm staying, too," Julie said.

"It's OK," Elizabeth said. "I'll try to catch up with you later."

Elizabeth watched Amy and Julie run to get on line. She would have liked to walk through the Blind Man's Bluff with them, but it was more important to Jessica, so she hurried off.

Four

◇

Elizabeth rushed across the park toward the Fun Zone, where the Super Coaster was located. Before she left Fairy Tale Land she glanced wistfully at the giant old-fashioned carousel right across the Plaza from Little Red Riding Hood's House. It was one of her favorite rides but she had no time to stop.

By the time she approached the Super Coaster, the entranceway was crowded. Elizabeth zig-zagged her way through to the front of the line. Narrowing her eyes, she scanned the crowd. A group of Sweet Valley kids had just climbed into the cars.

"Hey, Ken, Aaron," Elizabeth called. "Have either of you seen Jessica? Is she on the ride now?"

The boys didn't seem to hear her. They just grinned and waved as their car began to climb up the steep incline.

Elizabeth suddenly felt afraid that she'd never find Jessica in this large amusement park. Knots formed in her stomach as her worry grew. She took a deep breath. *Don't panic,* she told herself.

She weaved her way out of the line, sat down on a bench and tried to think.

There were a lot of people in the park now, but in spite of the crowd, Elizabeth had seen most of her classmates. Why hadn't she seen Jessica?

"Something's definitely wrong," Elizabeth said aloud. "I just feel it."

The last time she had actually seen Jessica was inside the castle ride. But she hadn't seen her get out of the boat. *That's weird,* Elizabeth thought. She shivered as a new worry suddenly made her feel cold.

What if she fell out of the boat? What if she's hurt? Poor Jess. All alone in the dark and no one to help her.

Elizabeth thought about searching for Mr. Bowman but then decided it would take too long to find him. She would just have to keep looking herself.

Wasting no time, she took off toward King Abelard's Castle. The distance between the rides seemed endless and the streets were crowded with people strolling along leisurely. Elizabeth wanted to run but it was impossible to move quickly.

At last she left the Fun Zone. Arriving back at Fairy Tale Land, she raced all the way to the castle ride's boat dock.

She gasped when she got to the door. Something was terribly wrong! No one was waiting on line. The boats were gone and no attendants were there. The castle itself sat strangely silent amid the silver eucalyptus trees.

More convinced than ever that the castle ride had something to do with Jessica's disappearance, Elizabeth searched for a way across the moat to the castle. She ran around looking for someone to help her.

She saw no one, but after a while she found a small row boat. Without thinking she quickly stepped inside and paddled over to the castle. Once she was ashore, she noticed a small door at the side of the gray building.

"How strange. I didn't notice that before," she said aloud. She walked closer, wondering if any of the ride attendants were inside.

She knocked lightly on the door but there was no answer. She reached forward and tried the knob. To her surprise, it turned easily. The door swung open. Inside Elizabeth saw a long corridor that disappeared into total darkness.

"Hello!" Elizabeth called. "Is anyone there?"

She heard only faint echoes of her own voice. She trembled at the thought of entering the dark corridor alone but knew that she must. How else could she find her twin?

"Jessica, hang on. I'm coming."

She took a deep breath and walked slowly through the door.

Five

◇

Within a few feet, Elizabeth found herself in total darkness. She suddenly remembered the skeletons she had seen earlier that morning and she almost screamed. What if one of those spooky visions reappeared suddenly in the darkness before her?

She took a few cautious steps, then stopped. A faint tremor echoed down the passageway. "Who's there?" she shouted.

No one answered.

Elizabeth was almost certain she heard the sound of metal clashing against metal, and . . . Was that a scream?

The smooth ground beneath her suddenly became rough and uneven. Elizabeth stumbled over a cobblestone but caught herself before she fell.

Certain she was imagining things, she took a

big step forward. The next thing she knew she was falling, falling . . . with nothing beneath her feet. With nothing to grab on to, Elizabeth tumbled down a steep incline. Slipping, then rolling, she scraped her elbow and her knee, crying out as she fell. At last she reached the bottom, where she collided with something big and heavy.

She sat up, rubbed her sore elbow, and looked around. At least there was more light down here. She seemed to be in a storeroom, and the object she had crashed into was a large wooden cask. Elizabeth's impact had knocked the cask onto its side, and out came a little girl!

"Who are *you*?" Elizabeth asked, unable to hide her surprise.

"My name is Princess Charity," the little girl answered, her face pale. "Are you one of them?"

"One of who? What are you talking about?" Elizabeth was more confused than ever.

"Quick," Princess Charity cried, glancing over her shoulder. "We must hide!"

"Hide from whom?" Elizabeth demanded.

"Can't you hear them?" the little girl asked. She looked back toward the darkness, her expression fearful.

Elizabeth listened. She could hear what sounded like swords clashing. It was the sound she had heard before.

"That's just part of the ride," she told Princess Charity.

The little girl shook her head and looked as if she might burst into tears. "King Nestor's knights will find us. They've already captured my parents and my brothers and put them into a cage with the rest of the kingdom."

"But the knights aren't real," Elizabeth tried to persuade the girl.

Charity shook her head stubbornly. "They're coming closer," she insisted.

Elizabeth stared at her. For the first time she noticed Charity's medieval clothes. The little girl wore a pink silk floor length tunic decorated with jewels and fine brocade. It was streaked with dirt and there were several tears in the lower part of the skirt.

"Are you part of the ride, too?" Elizabeth asked, then felt silly. The little girl was obviously as real as Elizabeth herself.

Maybe the attraction had added some actors and actresses, Elizabeth thought, observing how real the child's fear appeared. She seemed to tremble at every sound. Princess Charity certainly was a good actress!

But then Elizabeth looked down at Charity's hand and gasped. The little girl had a cut on her hand that dripped real blood. Even actresses didn't go so far as to get hurt for their parts.

What on earth was happening?

Elizabeth had no time to wonder. The sounds grew louder. Someone was approaching. Charity grabbed Elizabeth by the hand and pulled her into the big cask.

"Be quiet, or they'll hear," she whispered. She pulled the lid of the cask back into place. Elizabeth crouched beside her in the damp barrel. The smell inside was making her stomach churn. *This is impossible,* she thought to herself. *I must be part of a big play.* The whole situation seemed so silly, she wasn't even afraid.

The sound of footsteps near the cask interrupted her thoughts. A rough voice spoke briskly.

"Hold fast, my loyal page. The princess lies somewhere in the storehouse. Get on with it and bring her back to me."

"Yes, Prince Kendrick."

Charity trembled violently at the sound of the men's voices and Elizabeth was afraid the whole cask would shake along with her.

"For the honor of my father, King Nestor, I will find Princess Charity . . . or I'll die in the quest."

To seal his oath, the prince thrust the point of his broad sword into the lid of the cask. Elizabeth heard the swish of the metal blade as he swung it through the air, and she gasped as the sword splintered the wood right above her head.

The two girls clung to each other, waiting for the sword to come crashing through again.

"Methinks we should search the catacombs again," Kendrick said. "King Abelard's daughter surely knows her way around them."

"A princess hiding with the skeletons? What a fine sight that will be to see."

The two men laughed loudly and stomped off.

Inside the cask, Elizabeth breathed a deep sigh of relief.

When all was quiet outside, she pushed away the battered lid and crawled out. Charity followed. The princess sat down on the dirt floor and began to cry.

"Didn't I tell you?" she sobbed. "They're dreadful, dreadful men. They'll make me a slave if ever they find me."

"But you're just a child," Elizabeth exclaimed.

"It makes no difference to wicked King Nestor. He'll work me all day and keep me locked up all night. Then when I grow up he'll marry me off to his wretched son Kendrick, and I'll be miserable forever." Charity let the tears flow freely down her dirt-stained cheeks.

Elizabeth couldn't imagine how she had gotten into this situation. This was no play. But there was no point in trying to figure it out now. The child on the floor was obviously real and so were those evil knights. She would just have to find some way to help Charity get to her family and free them.

"How come your father didn't fight back?" Elizabeth asked.

Charity rubbed her bloodshot eyes. "He was taken by surprise," she said. "In the middle of our feast. He had no time to fight back."

"Well, then," Elizabeth said firmly, "we've got to give him that chance."

"But he's locked up inside a big cage," the young princess explained. "Along with my mother and brothers and scores of others from the kingdom. They can't possibly fight back from in there."

"Then we'll have to let them all out," Elizabeth said. "Where are their weapons?"

"King Nestor's knights collected all the swords and battle-axes and dumped them in the courtyard next to the cage.

"Good," Elizabeth said. "When you let them out, the king's defenders can grab their weapons and be ready to surprise the knights."

"Oh, I couldn't let them out," Charity said, gasping. "The knights would see me. They'd capture me for sure."

"Don't worry, I'm going to distract them," Elizabeth said.

"How?" Charity's deep brown eyes widened at Elizabeth's incredible daring.

"I don't know right now," Elizabeth confessed. "But I'll think of something!"

Six

◇

Elizabeth and Charity sat in silence on the dirt ground. Elizabeth refused to be discouraged.

"I *must* think of something to surprise the knights," she said. "Perhaps we could pile up these casks. When they fall, the knights will come running."

Charity looked doubtful. "But these casks are so heavy. I doubt the two of us could move them."

"I know! We could set something on fire. That would get their attention," Elizabeth suggested.

Charity shook her head. "Half the kingdom is on fire already," she pointed out.

Elizabeth's face fell. "Oh. Then I guess that won't work either. The knights wouldn't notice another fire."

This time the silence stretched for several minutes while Elizabeth searched her mind for a good plan. With each passing moment, Charity looked more and more miserable.

"It is no use," she wailed. "The knights will find me and take me away. I'll never see my family again."

"Hush," Elizabeth said. "We're not giving up yet. Please don't cry."

She patted the little girl on the shoulder. Charity continued to sniffle and Elizabeth reached into her pocket for a tissue to wipe away her tears. Alongside the tissue, she felt a hard, square object.

"My camera!" Elizabeth exclaimed. She had forgotten all about it. Pulling it out of her pocket she turned it over in her hand.

"Look," Elizabeth said, thinking it might make Charity stop crying. Hoping that her fall down the tunnel hadn't broken the mechanism, she aimed the small camera at Charity and snapped a picture. The flash popped in the little girl's face.

"Oh, great," Elizabeth said with relief. "It still works."

Charity covered her face with her hands, trembling from head to foot.

"Don't blind me!" she begged. "I thought you were my friend."

"I *am* your friend," Elizabeth said quickly. "Whatever made you think I'd want to blind you?"

Charity lowered her hands. She frowned at Elizabeth, her expression accusing. "You pointed that—that thing at me, and a great light appeared—just like a lightning bolt!"

"Oh, that." Elizabeth grinned. "That was the flash. Haven't you ever seen a camera before?"

The little girl shook her head, looking puzzled.

"Oh, well," Elizabeth said. "If any of this makes any sense, which it doesn't, I suppose you *wouldn't* know what a camera is. Hey! That gives me an idea!"

"What?" Charity asked.

"If you've never seen a camera flash, then neither have the knights. I'll use it to distract them! Let's make a plan. Can you draw me a map of your castle?"

They knelt together on the dirt floor. Charity took a twig and drew lines in the dirt, explaining the layout of the castle to Elizabeth.

"Here is where my people are being held," she explained pointing to a room off the center courtyard.

"And where are the knights?" Elizabeth asked.

"Over here." Charity made an X in the dirt.

"You must listen carefully," Elizabeth said. "We'll have only one chance."

Charity nodded as Elizabeth spoke. "I'll creep up to the cage and when the knights turn away, I'll unbar the door," she repeated after Elizabeth explained the plan.

"Right," Elizabeth said, putting one hand behind her back and crossing her fingers. "If only everything goes as planned! Let's go!"

Tiptoeing through the dark narrow pathways, Charity led the way back upstairs to the main hallway. Elizabeth marveled at the beautiful intricate tapestries all around her. It really was the castle from the ride come to life.

As they crept closer to the center of town, the shouts and swordplay grew louder. Elizabeth's knees felt weak, and her stomach still churned. Determined not to give in to her fear, she swallowed hard.

They peeked around the corner and entered the corridor that led to the central courtyard. Gingerly they stepped around broken pieces of glass that had been shattered by the invading knights. Then Elizabeth saw all the knights gathered around a big table in the middle of the courtyard. They seemed to be arguing over what to do with King Abelard and the rest of the prisoners.

"Look, there's my family over there," Charity whispered.

Elizabeth looked past the group of knights. There, on the other side of the courtyard, was the big wooden cage where the king and his people huddled.

"You'll have to slip behind these arches so no one sees you," Elizabeth told Charity. "When I distract the knights, run and open the cage door. Be careful. If the knights catch you, our whole plan will fail."

Charity's face turned pale, but she nodded.

"I'll count to one hundred to give you time to get into place," Elizabeth said. "Ready?"

Charity squeezed Elizabeth's hand, then slipped away into the shadows.

Elizabeth watched the knights as she counted silently. Prince Kendrick, King Nestor's son, stood in the center. His once-white frilled shirt was streaked with dirt and his tight black leggings were torn and frayed.

The men around him drank out of the same giant goblets Elizabeth remembered from the ride.

They were examining the loot they had stolen from the castle coffers. One man, still clad in his armor, clutched the queen's tiara, trying to pry off the diamonds with his dagger blade.

"Sixty-eight, sixty-nine, seventy," Elizabeth whispered. The seconds seemed to crawl by. Every time a knight looked up, Elizabeth trembled. She hoped Charity wouldn't be seen as she crept her way around the edge of the courtyard to the prisoners' cage.

"Seventy-eight, seventy-nine—" A sudden snort from behind made her heart stop. She froze, afraid it was a knight ready to capture her.

"Hee-haw." Elizabeth turned. A small, dusty, gray donkey tried to nibble on the sleeve of her T-shirt.

Elizabeth's relief only lasted a moment. What if the knights heard the noise?

"Go away," she whispered.

The donkey snorted again, then backed into the corridor that led to the stables. He kicked the wall. The noise echoed through the tall arches and one of the knights turned to see what was happening.

"Who's there?" he cried, his expression suspicious. He lifted his sword, eyeing the archway that sheltered Elizabeth.

"Oh no." Elizabeth gasped, trying to make herself invisible. "Go away, you stupid animal."

But the donkey didn't budge. A few more knights turned and stared right in her direction. Elizabeth was afraid to breathe.

"Come out!" the first knight commanded, stepping closer to Elizabeth's hiding place.

Elizabeth pushed the donkey hard. Snorting indignantly, the animal stepped out from behind the archway. The knight stared in surprise.

"Ho, Philip, are you afraid of an ass?" The other knights broke into uproarious laughter.

Elizabeth breathed a sigh of relief and continued counting. At last she reached one hundred. Praying that Charity was in position, Elizabeth gathered her courage and took out the small camera. Checking to see that it was ready to shoot, she stood up.

Her knees felt weak, and her hands trembled. But she stepped forward bravely. Within a few steps, one of the knights saw her.

"Ha," he cried, "another fair maiden for Nestor! Come along, girlie. 'Tis hopeless to run away."

Prince Kendrick turned to look at her. "Put her in the pen with the rest."

One knight started forward. Elizabeth held up one hand to stop him, then cleared her throat.

"Wait," she shouted. "I have a weapon more powerful than all of your blades and arrows."

Disbelieving, a few of the knights approached her. She raised her small camera quickly. "You'll see," she cried. "It will paralyze all of you where you stand."

She squeezed the shutter button. The flash's bright light flared. The knights stood stock-still and several cried out.

"My eyes! I can't see."

"I'm blinded!"

While they hesitated, Elizabeth saw Charity run toward the prisoners' cage. Determined to keep the knights from looking back that way, she continued her charade.

"Don't move," she warned. She flashed the camera twice in quick succession.

The knights stood dumbfounded.

But Prince Kendrick wasn't fooled. "We're not dead, you fools," he growled. "Now take the girl and put her in the cage!"

When no one else dared to move, he dropped the jewelry that filled his wide hands and stalked toward Elizabeth. He drew his sword and raised it high above her head.

Before he could take a swing, a man crept up

from behind and brought a heavy mace crashing down on his head. Prince Kendrick crumpled to the ground with hardly a grunt.

"Thank you, sir!" Elizabeth cried.

The big man grinned. But another knight ran toward him, and he lifted his sword with no time to reply. Elizabeth slipped back into the shadow of the archway and watched as the kingdom-dwellers seized their stolen weapons and attacked the evil knights.

Within a few minutes the last of the wicked invaders had been overcome. King Abelard's own knights dragged them away and locked them into the cage that had once been their own prison.

At last they were free. And Elizabeth had helped!

Seven

"Thank goodness you're safe!"

Elizabeth spun around and was quickly embraced by Charity. "How about you?" she asked the girl. "Are you all right?"

Charity beamed. "I'm fine, and I have my family back, thanks to you."

With their prisoners secure and their wounds tended to, the other members of the kingdom gathered around the two girls.

"Here is the brave maiden who saved us all," one of the men shouted.

Elizabeth blushed. "I only did what anyone would do," she told them. "And Charity helped. I'm just glad our plan worked."

An old woman stared at her closely. "But child, how did you get away? I thought I saw you captured earlier by that wretched King Nestor."

Elizabeth gasped. "That must have been my twin sister, Jessica. She looks just like me," she explained. "I've been trying to find her. Do you know where they took her?"

"I heard them say that she was being taken back to his kingdom. There's a boy on the other side of the forest with a raft. He could take you there."

King Abelard himself offered to guide Elizabeth to the other side of the forest and she accepted gratefully. She gave Charity one last hug, then turned to follow the king into the dark woods.

The trail they took dipped close to the water's edge and passed under tall pine trees whose fallen needles crunched under the weight of their footsteps. Elizabeth was very glad to have the king's help.

Eventually the path sloped toward higher ground, and the pines gave way to a meadow bright with blooming wildflowers. They stopped at the crest of a small hill.

"You can't get lost from here," the king told Elizabeth. "Go straight down the hill to the old dock at the water's edge. There you will find the boy's raft. He'll not be far away."

"Thank you so much," Elizabeth said. She waved as the king turned back toward his castle, then she marched briskly down the hill. Soon she came to the river and the old wooden dock. At the far end, a much-mended fishnet had been spread out to dry in the sun. A log raft was tied to one end of the dock, where it bobbed in the water. But no boy was in sight.

Elizabeth walked along the riverbank, hoping to find a sign of the raft's owner. When she rounded the next bend, she came upon a boy stretched out on the grass. A straw hat covered his face and a fishing pole stuck in the sand beside him stretched its line into the shifting water.

"Well," Elizabeth said, trying not to giggle. "How many fish do you think you'll catch that way?"

At the sound of her voice, the boy stirred. He lifted a hand to push aside the straw hat.

Elizabeth saw a pleasant freckled face, with clear blue eyes, a tiny upturned nose, and sandy hair tousled from his nap. The boy wore a striped shirt and blue cotton trousers rolled up to just below his knees. His feet were bare, brown from the sun and slightly scratched.

He sat up and blinked at Elizabeth, his mouth hanging open in surprise.

"I know I must look strange to you," she said. "These clothes . . ."

But the boy shook his head, at last closing his mouth and looking more alert. "You don't look strange," he said. "You look beautiful. You have hair like spun gold, and eyes the color of a rushing river."

"Oh." Elizabeth blushed. "Thank you. Can you help me? King Abelard told me you might be able to take me to King Nestor's kingdom."

"Whatever for?" the boy asked, frowning just a little. "He's a mean one."

"But that's where they took my sister," Elizabeth explained. "I have to save her. Can we go there on your raft?"

"Of course," the boy said gallantly, jumping to his feet.

Elizabeth discovered that he was slightly taller than she was. She smiled at him.

"Thank you so much. My name is Elizabeth."

The boy reached to pull off his hat, remembered it was still lying on the grass, and grinned instead. "Mine's Tom Sawyer," he told her.

It was Elizabeth's turn to gape. *Tom Sawyer?* This was incredible.

She felt like pinching herself to make sure she

wasn't dreaming. First a terrifying encounter with medieval knights, and now a chance to sail down the river with Tom Sawyer!

Tom pulled up his fishing pole and picked up his straw hat, and together they walked back to the dock.

"Don't you go to school?" Elizabeth asked Tom.

"Not when I can get out of it," Tom said, grinning slyly. "And when I do go, I'm so much trouble, the schoolmaster's glad when I play truant again."

Elizabeth giggled. "You won't learn anything if you keep that up," she told him.

Tom looked embarrassed. "I study hard," he assured her. "I've been head of the class lots of times. But I also know the river," he continued. "There's a lot to learn outdoors, too."

They came to the dock and boarded the small raft. Elizabeth stepped cautiously onto the shifting boards, feeling them sway beneath her weight.

"Sit here in the middle. It's safest," Tom observed, watching her.

Elizabeth knelt on the rough logs. Tom untied the raft, then stepped to the rear and took hold of the long pole that he used to steer it.

They drifted away from the dock, slowly at first,

then rapidly once they got caught up in the river's swift current.

Elizabeth swallowed hard, watching the rolling water all around them. She wouldn't want to be thrown into those waves. She was thankful to see that Tom held his rudder easily and appeared confident and relaxed.

"You're good at this," she told him. "You really know the river."

"Yup," he agreed. He looked so pleased with her praise that Elizabeth giggled again.

"You sure are pretty," he told her.

Elizabeth turned away from his adoring gaze. She was pleased by his obvious admiration, but she wasn't sure how to respond. She suddenly thought of her twin. *Jessica would know what to say to him.*

"Who did you say you were looking for?" Tom asked.

"My sister Jessica," Elizabeth answered.

"Oh." He nodded. "I have a sister, too. She bosses me around a lot."

"Jessica tries that sometimes," Elizabeth said. "And sometimes I get angry at her." She let out a loud sigh, remembering their quarrel. "But I still love her." If only she could tell Jessica that in person.

Tom grinned. "Me and my friend Huck play tricks on the girls sometimes. I slipped a frog in my sister Mary's sewing basket once. You should have heard her yell."

They both laughed.

"I bet you and Huck have great times together," Elizabeth observed. Who would ever have imagined that she would be having such a conversation with Tom Sawyer? She still couldn't believe her good luck.

"Does he go rafting with you?" she asked, hoping for more stories.

Tom nodded. "Sometimes. But he's not around today. Anyhow," he told her, "you wouldn't like him. He gets into more trouble than me, and he hates to take baths."

Elizabeth giggled again. How could Tom be jealous of Huckleberry Finn? She hadn't even met him! "If you say so," she said. "What about Becky Thatcher?"

Tom stared at her. "You know Becky?"

"I've heard of her," Elizabeth answered cautiously. "Isn't she your girlfriend?"

Tom turned red. "Naw," he said stoutly. "Not anymore; that was when we were just young 'uns.

When we got lost in the big cave, and Injun Joe almost killed us."

"Tell me about it," Elizabeth begged.

Tom needed little encouragement. "I know that cave inside and out," he bragged. "But Becky wanted to go real far inside, you know? And then our candles burnt out, and it was as dark as a bat's cellar."

Elizabeth nodded, eager to hear Tom's story from his own lips. "You must have been terrified."

"Not me." Tom shrugged. "Becky was a mite scared, I reckon. We felt our way through the dark, wondering if we'd starve to death before we could find our way out. And then Injun Joe popped up. I thought we were goners for sure!"

Elizabeth's eyes widened, even though she knew the end of the story. She'd just finished reading *Tom Sawyer* a few days earlier.

"But we—*I* outsmarted him," Tom said. "We slipped out another tunnel, and Injun Joe was trapped inside!"

Elizabeth couldn't keep from clapping.

"That's great, Tom," she cried. "Even better than the book."

"What book?" he asked, looking surprised.

"Oh, just a book I read once," Elizabeth told him quickly.

"There's nothing like *my* story in a book," he said. "But books are grand, aren't they? I read *Robin Hood* three times."

Tom looked up and pointed toward a small hill that rose out of the river. "There it is—Nestor's kingdom." He began to steer the raft toward the barren-looking land.

They arrived with a jolt against the rocky shore. Tom quickly threw his rope around a lone big oak near the water's edge, tying the raft safely to its stout trunk. Then he and Elizabeth jumped ashore.

"Where do you think your sister could be?" Tom asked.

Elizabeth looked perplexed. "I'm not sure," she confessed. "I'll just have to start searching."

"I'll help you," Tom offered. They both started up the grassy slope.

The rolling, rocky hills before them appeared to be deserted. A robin flew out of a berry bush, and a small brown wren scolded them for disturbing the thicket. But there was no sign of any people.

"I hope this is the right place," Elizabeth said.

Tom, who had walked ahead of her, called over his shoulder, "Look!"

Elizabeth ran to join him. Looking down where he pointed, she saw a footprint in the sandy soil.

"Someone has been here," she cried.

"This way," Tom told her. They hurried on. Soon they came out of the trees and brush and found themselves at the bottom of a small hill. The trail seemed to end there. Tom dropped to his knees and examined the ground carefully for signs. "Over here," he said.

Elizabeth came closer, looking over the bare rocky hillside. "What's that?" she asked.

Tom stood up. His sandy brows rose in surprise. "It's a cave," he exclaimed. "I've never seen this one before."

The small opening in the side of the hill was barely big enough to admit them. They squeezed through and found that the opening soon widened. A large cavern led back into the hill.

"Look." Tom pointed to fresh-tracked dirt on the rocky floor of the cave. "Someone's been inside, all right."

"Then we have to keep going," Elizabeth said, although the thought of venturing deeper into the dark interior made her shiver.

Side by side they walked further into the cavern. Tom took a short candle out of his pocket and lit it.

They followed the wavering light carefully, skirting a couple of deep pits. A small stream ran along the side of the cave. Although only a few inches deep, it made the air even more cool and damp.

A sudden sound broke the silence, like a faraway cry.

Elizabeth lifted her head, straining to hear.

"What was that?" she whispered, waiting for the faint noise to be repeated.

"I'm not sure," Tom admitted.

Elizabeth shivered. "It sounded almost like a girl screaming! Oh, Tom, what if it's Jessica!"

Elizabeth ran forward, too impatient to stay within the circle of flickering light. Tom hurried to catch up with her.

Then something swooped down out of the darkness and brushed Elizabeth's hair. She shrieked.

"It's only a bat," Tom told her calmly.

"A bat?" Elizabeth, afraid the creature would tangle its wide wings in her hair, ran wildly until she tripped over a small pile of rocks. As she stumbled to her knees, Tom hurried forward to help her.

"Look out!" he yelled.

With an ominous rumbling, the wall of the cave started to crumble. A great wave of stone rushed forward to engulf them both.

Eight

◇

Tom grabbed Elizabeth's hand and pulled her back, but the rockfall moved too swiftly. Losing their footing, they fell in a heap. The slide of rocks and dirt seemed to go on forever. Elizabeth and Tom huddled close to the floor of the cave, covering their heads with their arms. Elizabeth coughed, choked by the cloud of dust that accompanied the falling rocks.

At last the rumbling stopped. "Tom?" Elizabeth cried. "Are you all right?"

A muffled cough was her only answer, but Elizabeth's worry faded a bit. At least he was still breathing. She heard the faint scrape of a match being struck, and then a tiny flame appeared in the darkness as Tom relit his candle. Elizabeth took a deep breath and looked around. The rockslide had completely cut off their exit. They were trapped in a small area of the cave, with no way out!

Elizabeth shook her head.

"Tom," she said, "I'm really sorry I got you into this."

"Heck," Tom said, shrugging. "What are friends for? I couldn't let you go by yourself, could I? Would Robin Hood desert his merry men?"

Elizabeth laughed. "I guess not. Thanks."

"Tell you something else," Tom said. "Know that pile of rocks you tripped over?"

"The one that started the whole rockslide?" Elizabeth nodded, feeling another stab of guilt. "I know, it was my fault. I'm so sorry. I shouldn't have run ahead like that."

Tom shook his head. "It wasn't your fault, Elizabeth. Just before the candle went out, I saw a rope attached to the pile of rocks. I think someone deliberately set a booby trap for anyone coming into the cave."

Elizabeth gasped. "That's really awful, Tom. Who do you think did it?"

"King Nestor. I told you he was a bad one," he said.

Elizabeth shivered. If Jessica were in the hands of someone as evil as that, what might be happening to her right now? "I hope my sister's all right." Elizabeth's voice broke slightly as she tried not to cry.

Tom patted her on the shoulder. "You're awfully fond of her, aren't you?"

Elizabeth nodded. "We have our differences, but I wouldn't want anything bad to happen to her. I feel so guilty."

"What for?" Tom looked concerned.

Elizabeth thought of how Jessica had tried to speak to her before the castle ride. It seemed like a million years had passed since then. If only Elizabeth had allowed Jessica to sit with her she might never have disappeared.

"Don't look so sad," Tom said. "You've been really brave to track your sister this far. Don't give up. We'll find her."

Elizabeth smiled at Tom's optimism. She hoped he was right. But how would they ever get out of their rocky prison?

Elizabeth walked closer to examine the wall of stones that trapped them. She stepped into something cold and looked down in surprise.

"What's this?"

Tom let out a long whistle.

The little trickle of water they had seen earlier had been affected by the rockfall. The water had no place to go and was rapidly forming a pool. The small stream had doubled in size.

"Oh, Tom," Elizabeth said. "We'll drown if this gets too deep!"

She backed away from the water toward the other side of the cave. Something small scurried over her feet, making her jump.

"Yikes!" Elizabeth yelled.

"That's just a mouse," Tom said. He picked up a small rock and took aim. "I'll kill it."

"No, don't," Elizabeth said quickly. "I'm not afraid of mice, really. It just startled me, and I didn't know what it was."

They both stood back against the cave wall, watching the dark pool of water grow deeper.

"Oh, Tom, what will we do?" Elizabeth said. She studied the stone wall created by the rockslide and narrowed her gaze. "Wait! Look at that top rock. It seems to be holding the whole stack in place. And it really doesn't seem very steady. If we could move it, I think the pile might shift again and we'd find a way out."

Tom lifted his candle. They stared at the big rock. "I think you're right," he said. "Here, you hold this."

Elizabeth took the candle from Tom. It was awfully short. When it melted, they'd be completely in the dark. She realized they didn't have much time.

Tom felt around the cave floor and collected a pile of small rocks. Then he hefted a fist-sized rock, took aim, and threw it at the rock on top of the pile. It missed. He muttered in disgust, then selected a second rock. This time he hit the big rock squarely. It seemed to shake, but the impact wasn't strong enough to topple it from the stack.

Tom hit the rock several more times, but none of the blows was forceful enough to push it out of place. He looked so upset that Elizabeth tried to reassure him.

"It's not your fault," she told him. "You hit it perfectly. These rocks just aren't heavy enough."

The pool of water now lapped at their feet and the candle was almost down to its last inch. Elizabeth gulped. She had never thought she would die so young. And like this—so far from home. What would her parents and Steven think when she didn't return? Would they ever find her?

Elizabeth felt tears at the corners of her eyes. A giant lump in her throat made it hard to swallow. What about Jessica? Who would save her now?

"Tom," she said. "I didn't mean to get you into this mess."

He took her hand. "I wouldn't have missed it," he said gallantly. "I like a good adventure now and then."

Elizabeth tried to smile, although the lump in her throat still ached. Suddenly a flicker of movement near the wall of rocks caught her eye. Something small and dark was scampering up the stones.

"Look!" she cried. "It's the mouse. What's it doing?" Clinging to the side of the cave, the little animal reached the top of the untidy stack of rocks. Then they heard the sound of gnawing.

Elizabeth blinked in surprise. "It's chewing on that clump of grass stuck under the big rock," she said. "Do you think—"

A sudden surge of water swept up to her knees, startling her. The water was freezing cold.

"Do you think the mouse can do what we couldn't?" She hardly dared to hope. The mouse was so small, and the rock so big.

The little animal continued to chew on the grass beneath the rock. Tom and Elizabeth watched anxiously as the water crept up to their thighs.

Elizabeth held the candle high. The water now reached her waist. Soon it would be too late.

But just as the water was about to cover them completely, the mouse severed the last strand of grass. No longer lodged securely, the big rock began to slide.

"It's moving!" Tom yelled. "Look out!"

Sure enough, as soon as the top rock slipped out of place, the whole wall of stones began to slide. Elizabeth pushed her way through the cold water, but she couldn't move fast enough. It was impossible to avoid the falling rock. She felt sharp blows on her arms and shoulders.

As the rocks splashed into the pool, the candle went out, plunging the cave into total darkness.

The rocks continued to crash all around them. Elizabeth, losing Tom's comforting grip, tried to push her way to safety.

As the rock wall crumpled, she felt the water swirl around her, then disappear. Still shivering in her wet clothes, she scrambled to a drier perch.

When the last echoes of the rockslide died, Elizabeth couldn't believe she was safe. She stretched her arms and legs carefully. She was still damp and cold, and her bruises ached, but no bones seemed broken. But where was Tom?

"Tom?" she called. "Are you all right?"

Nine

◇

The darkness and the silence were almost too much for Elizabeth to take. Just as panic was about to overcome her, she heard Tom's voice. "I'm all right. Where are you?"

"I don't know," Elizabeth said.

"Follow my voice, but move slowly," Tom advised her.

Good idea, Elizabeth thought. She didn't want to risk another rockslide. "I will. But say something."

"Let me think—'When in the course of human events . . .'"

Elizabeth grinned at his choice. "Very good," she told him.

"Yes," Tom agreed, not very modestly. "I won an oratory contest at school once with the Declaration of Independence."

As Tom continued to recite, Elizabeth crawled

over the rock-strewn cave floor toward his voice. She was alarmed to encounter another wall of stone.

"Tom," she called. "You're on the other side of the rocks!"

"Of course." He sounded surprised. "This is the way back to the entrance. Where are you?"

Elizabeth shook her head, though she knew that her friend couldn't see her. "I must have jumped the other way when the stones came down. Now what?"

They both felt along the loosely piled stones. Tom tried to move some of the rocks, but there were too many. The barrier was complete.

"It's no use," he said. "I'll have to go back this way. What about you? Can you see any light from the other end of the cave?"

Elizabeth hadn't even noticed that her eyes had gradually adjusted to the faint light. She could make out shadowy outlines of the cave walls. She looked over her shoulder.

"I can, Tom," she said. "I think there's light coming from the other end of the tunnel. There must be another exit. I've got to try to find my sister," she called. "Go on back to your raft, Tom. I can go on from here. I've gotten you into enough trouble already."

"Heck, trouble's my middle name," Tom assured her. "But if you really want me to go . . ."

She heard a trace of sadness in his voice, and she felt sad, too. She probably wouldn't see him again.

"Go ahead," she said. "You've been a great help, Tom. I couldn't have made it this far without you. But now I have to go on by myself. I'll never forget meeting you."

"Me neither," Tom asserted. "And you're lots prettier than Becky Thatcher."

Elizabeth giggled. "Thank you. Take care, Tom."

"I hope you find your sister," Tom said. "Good-bye."

"Good-bye," Elizabeth called. She turned toward the far end of the tunnel and began to make her way slowly along the rocky floor. As she crept through the narrow cave, Elizabeth couldn't help feeling very alone. Tom had been a good friend. Would she really be able to rescue Jessica all by herself? Who knew what kind of evil person had kidnapped her twin?

Elizabeth kept going until she saw a small circle of light up ahead in the distance. As she came closer, the circle grew, and at last she found the opening she'd hoped for. She ran the last few feet and emerged onto a rocky plain.

"Hooray!" she cried, waving her arms in the open air.

Her happiness was short-lived. It was nighttime. A full moon shone brightly from the sky, casting light all around. Elizabeth had no idea how long she and Tom had been inside the cave, but it seemed like days.

Rocks littered the ground, and scrawny bushes cast dark shadows. With no hint of where her sister had been taken, and no Tom to help her look for tracks, how could Elizabeth hope to follow her twin?

She knelt on the hard ground, searching for tracks as Tom had done. She could detect nothing but hard-packed dirt and a few blades of tough grass. She stood up again and turned in a slow circle. Now what?

Just as Elizabeth thought her quest was truly hopeless, she heard a faint cry.

"Help me," the voice cried.

"Jessica?" Elizabeth yelled. "Where are you?"

A sob was her only answer. But from where? Elizabeth shut her eyes and tried to place it. Again she heard a faraway cry, and now she was certain. It came from the sky!

Elizabeth looked up. What she saw astonished her. Broad moonbeams stretched down to where she was standing. They appeared solid, like a pathway into the sky.

That's impossible, Elizabeth thought. Yet at the end of the silver path she could make out two tiny figures. One of them, dragged along by the taller form, had long blond hair!

"Jessica!" Elizabeth called.

She was answered with a whimpering cry. Then the two figures went over a cloud and dropped out of sight.

"What can I do?" Elizabeth cried. "This is ridiculous. I can't walk up a moonbeam."

"How will you know unless you try?" A small thin voice asked.

Elizabeth jumped. She looked down at the ground and saw a tiny animal at her feet. She stepped back quickly.

"I'm not going to bite you," the voice said.

She bent over to take a closer look. It was the little mouse from the cave! And it was a girl! *Mice can't talk*, she thought. *Can they?*

She didn't look like an ordinary mouse. She stood up on her hind legs, and even had a smile on her face. And how odd. She was wearing a little pink dress!

Elizabeth grinned. "Do you have a name?"

"Allegra," the mouse answered, giving her a dainty bow. "Pleased to meet you."

Why shouldn't Elizabeth be standing in the middle of nowhere talking to a mouse? Nothing else seemed normal in her life anymore.

"My name is Elizabeth," she told the little rodent. "I'm trying to rescue my twin sister, Jessica. She's been kidnapped, first by King Nestor, and now by—somebody, I'm not really sure whom."

"Why, that's terrible," Allegra said. "We've got to save her."

"I'm trying to," Elizabeth said. "But how can I walk up a path made of moonbeams?"

"You just do it," Allegra said. "Put me in your pocket and we'll go together. Hasn't anyone ever told you you should always try three impossible things before breakfast?"

"But I've had my breakfast already," Elizabeth said with a grin. "And I think I've done at least three impossible things already today. But it's worth a try. So let's get going, Allegra."

She bent over and put out her hand so the mouse could walk onto her palm. She placed her carefully into her T-shirt pocket.

"OK. Now shut your eyes and take three steps forward," Allegra instructed.

Elizabeth did as instructed. On the last step she was astonished to feel her feet touching a soft surface that wobbled slightly beneath her.

She opened her eyes, looked down, and gasped. They were several feet off the ground. For a moment Elizabeth was too frightened to move. She was sure they would sink through the misty moonbeam and fall to the ground.

"What are you waiting for?" Allegra called impatiently. "We'll never catch up with your sister if you stop to sightsee!"

Elizabeth took another step. It was like walking on a trampoline. "Jessica, I'm coming!" she cried, her courage returning. With a glance down at the mouse in her pocket, she broke into a run and raced up the moonbeam path.

Ten

◇

Elizabeth had never taken such a marvelous walk. She bounced a little with each passing step, and the moonbeam shimmered beneath her feet. She skipped, her spirits higher than they'd been since this strange journey began. Soon she'd be reunited with her sister.

She walked up to the highest point of the moonbeam, where the air suddenly grew chilly and damp. She stood still for a moment, and a soft mist rolled around her. She could no longer see where the path led.

"What happened?" Allegra asked, peeking out of her pocket. "Who turned on the shower? I'm getting soaked."

"I think we walked into a cloud," Elizabeth said. "I can't see our moonbeam anymore. I don't know which way to go."

Allegra wiped the water out of her eyes, and they both peered into the fog. A dull thumping noise vibrated through the mist.

"Follow the sound," Allegra advised. "But go carefully."

Elizabeth didn't need the warning. She tiptoed cautiously through the mist until she felt more solid footing beneath her.

"I think we've arrived," she whispered to the mouse. "I just don't know where!"

In another moment the mist around them lifted, and Elizabeth was able to look around.

The moonbeam had disappeared. They stood before a tall stone fence with a large gray gate. "I wonder if it's locked," Elizabeth said.

She approached cautiously and pulled on the heavy gate. It opened just wide enough to admit her, and with Allegra still in her pocket, she stepped inside.

They entered a completely different world. The ground was level and stretched into the distance toward large, barren mountains that rose against the horizon. The light was neither the golden sunlight of a normal day nor the silvery moonlit night Elizabeth and Allegra had left behind. Instead it was gray, like an eternal twilight.

In fact everything was gray. Elizabeth's optimism vanished. She saw no sign of green, nothing growing, no sparkle of blue water. There weren't even white clouds in the sky anymore.

She saw movement in the distance. When she and Allegra got closer, she could see men, women, and children bent over shovels and picks like farm laborers. But instead of tilling rich earth or tending planted fields, they were cracking huge gray boulders into smaller stones.

"What on earth are they doing?" she wondered.

She slowed to a walk and peered at the people around her dressed in drab gray uniforms. No one looked up, no one questioned the stranger in their midst. Their expressions were sullen and hopeless. Worse yet, except for the crack of picks against rocks, they worked in silence.

"This is an awful place," Elizabeth whispered to Allegra.

"Look," the tiny mouse said. "They're chained."

Elizabeth gasped. It was true. All the people wore sturdy metal bands around their legs, and the big chains led to heavy lead balls.

"No wonder they can't run away," Elizabeth groaned. "Oh, where is Jessica? Is she a slave, too?"

"Does she have blond hair, like you?" Allegra asked.

"Yes," Elizabeth nodded. "She looks just like me."

"I think I see her," Allegra announced.

Elizabeth whirled to look. "Jessica!" She ran toward her twin, who held a pick, just like everyone else. "I've come to rescue you!" Elizabeth cried.

To her surprise, Jessica hardly looked up. Instead of being surprised or happy, Jessica continued to bang away at her own large rock, and the gloomy look on her face didn't change.

"I don't know why you came," she muttered. "If I'm such a bad sister, why do you want me back?"

Elizabeth was shocked. She flung her arms around her sister and hugged her. "Oh, Jessica, this whole thing was all my fault. I shouldn't have ignored you. Besides, if you love someone, you love her even when she's not perfect. Especially your own twin sister!"

Hope flickered across Jessica's face. "Really?" she questioned her sister. "Even when I'm selfish?"

"Of course. I'd love you no matter what you did," Elizabeth insisted. "Although it wouldn't hurt you to *try* to keep your promises," she couldn't resist adding.

"It's no use." Jessica looked down at her chains. "I'm stuck here."

"We'll use your pick to break the chains and free you," Elizabeth told her.

"It won't work. The chains are magic," Jessica explained with a sigh. Her blue eyes looked dull and she seemed to have forgotten how to smile.

But Elizabeth wasn't convinced. "What on earth are all these people doing, anyhow?" she asked. "And who brought you here?"

"It's the Queen of Drudgery," Jessica said. "She bought me from King Nestor. Her prisoners have to work forever cracking big rocks into little rocks, and little rocks into gravel. The queen covers everything with gravel so that nothing will grow. She hates anything beautiful. She wants the whole world gray and drab and plain. She doesn't like happy people. They give her a headache."

"What an awful person," Elizabeth said, shocked. "We have to do something."

Jessica shook her head. "It's hopeless," she said, lifting her pick for another swing at the rock.

Elizabeth looked down into her pocket. "What can we do, Allegra?"

The little animal shook her head. "This is powerful magic," she admitted sadly. "I don't know how to break the queen's spell."

"We have to try," Elizabeth cried. Her voice echoed over the silent plain. "I'll find the queen."

"It's too late." Allegra shook her head. "I think she's already found you." She pointed down to the ground.

Elizabeth looked down, and her face paled. A manacle had formed around her own foot. As she watched, the heavy links began to grow. She had no doubt they would soon lead to a heavy ball. She was a prisoner, too!

"Oh no," Elizabeth moaned. "Now what are we going to do?"

Someone chuckled behind them. The chill, evil laughter made Elizabeth's skin crawl. She tried to turn quickly and almost fell over her chain. Catching herself, she gazed at the woman who had made the awful sound.

She was tall, thin and dressed all in gray, with limp hair and eyes that seemed almost transparent. She wore a gray crown that, on closer inspection, was formed from interwoven chains.

Elizabeth trembled at the sight. Jessica also

looked frightened. Allegra crouched down in Elizabeth's pocket where she couldn't be seen.

"Another slave for my stone pits," the queen chortled. "Have a shovel, my dear."

A long, gray shovel appeared suddenly in front of Elizabeth.

"I won't," Elizabeth said, her voice defiant. She lifted her head to meet the horrid queen's gaze.

"Ho, ho." The queen laughed. "Such spirit. This one will make a strong worker, indeed."

The gray shovel jumped off the hard ground and into Elizabeth's hands. She tried to throw it down, but the shaft stuck to her hands as if attached with glue. "I can't let go!" Elizabeth cried.

The queen let out another evil chuckle. "That's right, dear. Now get to work."

"That's what *you* think," Elizabeth retorted. She tried to swing the heavy shovel at the queen's head, but the chain around her ankle held her back. The shovel swung uselessly through the air without coming near the hateful woman.

Elizabeth groaned. She was trapped.

"I'm sorry, Lizzie," Jessica called, her voice forlorn. "It's all because of me. You shouldn't have come."

"You're my sister, Jess. We have to stand up for each other. We're not going to let her get away with this," Elizabeth cried.

The queen continued to chuckle.

Elizabeth didn't know what to do. "Can't anyone help us?" she cried.

As if in response, a clear, high note suddenly vibrated through the air. It was the first pleasant sound Elizabeth had heard in the wicked queen's kingdom.

The evil queen put both her hands to her ears, a look of pain on her face. "Look," Allegra whispered from her pocket. "Up in the sky."

Elizabeth lifted her gaze toward a dot in the gray sky. What was it?

The dot came closer and closer, until she could make out a black shape, As it neared, Elizabeth gaped in surprise. It was a black limousine with large white wings on its sides. Echoing the same clear notes, it continued to zoom closer.

Was this a friend or one of the queen's wicked aides? Elizabeth noted that the queen eyed the strange vehicle with a look of fear.

Her hope returned. She watched the car glide to a stop on the surface of the planet, crunching noisily on the gravel surface as its clear music faded. A red-capped chauffeur got out and opened one of the rear doors. Out stepped a face so familiar that Elizabeth felt her heart flutter. She must be mistaken.

Could it really be Johnny Buck?

Eleven

◇

Elizabeth's knees felt weak. She sat down abruptly, hardly noticing the roughness of the gravel beneath her. Were her eyes playing tricks on her? How could Johnny Buck, her very favorite singer, suddenly show up in this strange place?

Then she remembered that she was locked in magic chains and holding a talking mouse in her pocket.

It certainly looked like the famous rock singer. The slender, blond-haired teen was dressed in a dazzling outfit that contrasted sharply with the gray landscape. His white leather jumpsuit was fringed in white and purple and he wore long purple suede gloves and boots. *Jessica's favorite color*, Elizabeth noted.

She remembered the time, not that long ago, when Jessica had defied their parents and snuck out of the house to see Johnny Buck in concert. She could just imagine how her twin must be feeling right now, with Johnny just a few steps away. She turned to Jessica and was shocked to see her stony, expressionless face. She didn't seem to care at all. And he was walking right in their direction!

Too late Elizabeth remembered the danger he faced.

"Johnny," she called. "Go back to your limo. The queen has magic spells. If you come any closer you'll be put in chains like everyone else."

But his blue eyes were calm as he approached the tall gray queen. He faced her without fear.

"Another healthy young slave for my rock pits," she cooed. "This is a profitable day, indeed."

Johnny's expression was grave. "Stop this cruel practice right now," he told the queen in a clear, strong voice. "You have no right to enslave other human beings."

"Ho, ho," the queen chuckled. "What a cocky young man! I shall enjoy seeing you in chains."

"Oh, Johnny," Elizabeth moaned. "I told you not to come. Look!"

She could hardly bear to watch the magic manacle forming around the young man's ankle. Another slave for the wicked queen!

But Johnny didn't bother to look down. "I gave you your chance," he told the queen. Without waiting for her to speak, he began to sing.

The queen shuddered and put her hands over her ears. "Stop that at once!" she commanded. "Stop that terrible noise!"

Johnny ignored her command and went on singing. The song he sang was so lilting and happy that Elizabeth couldn't help smiling.

Then, to her delight, the magic shovel suddenly dropped from her hands. "Johnny," she cried. "It's working! Don't stop!"

His clear, liquid notes drifted across the gray land. The other slaves lifted their heads, and their hopeless expressions changed into smiles. They stopped swinging their picks and shovels and began to move to the beat of the music.

"Louder!" Elizabeth encouraged.

Johnny's new song was even faster and more spirited. The magic picks and shovels dropped from the enslaved workers' hands. They began to clap and sing along with him and as they did, their manacles and chains disappeared.

The gray queen still covered her ears. There was a look of pain on her face, and her shoulders were stooped as if to protect her from the music.

"You nasty girl," she snarled at Elizabeth. "You started this rebellion!"

The gray, drab costumes of the former slaves began to change color as the queen's magic lost its power. Now dressed in bright shades of every color of the rainbow, the crowd came closer to glare at the wicked queen. She backed away from the angry mob as she cast a vengeful glance toward Elizabeth. "It's all your fault," she croaked. "You'll pay for this."

"I only came to save my sister," Elizabeth protested.

She turned to look at her twin. Jessica had also dropped her pick and was staring in surprise at the chain that no longer hampered her movements.

"I'm free," Jessica cried out happily. "Oh, Elizabeth, you did it after all! And look, there's Johnny Buck!" She started to run to him, but the Queen of Drudgery stopped her.

"No, you don't," she cackled. "I've decided to keep one of my slaves—and I think it should be you, dear."

Elizabeth watched in horror as the gray queen threw Jessica over her shoulder and ran quickly across the rocky ground.

Elizabeth tried to run after her, but a dozen large rocks rose from the gravel-covered ground, making her stumble. She fell to her knees, crying out as the rough rocks scraped her skin.

A great boulder in front of her abruptly sprouted legs and wobbled to the queen's aid. Elizabeth, still on her knees, watched helplessly as the queen, still holding on to Jessica, rapped on its side. A door appeared suddenly, and the queen and her captive entered the now-hollow sphere.

"Jessica!" Elizabeth shouted.

Jessica waved frantically at her sister, but she couldn't break away. The big gray rock vessel pulled in its legs, sprouted wings, and began to lift off the ground.

"Oh no," Elizabeth moaned, watching it sail slowly into the sky. She was losing her sister all over again!

Twelve

◇

Elizabeth watched in dismay as the gray boulder rose higher and higher.

"Jessica!" she cried.

But Jessica could only wave helplessly from the window of the magical craft while the gray queen shook with evil laughter beside her.

Elizabeth ran back toward the black limousine. The rest of the freed slaves had gathered around Johnny to thank him. "Johnny," she called, pushing her way through the crowd. "The queen took my sister. Please help me! We can't leave her in the hands of that awful woman."

Her voice broke as she swallowed a sob.

"Don't cry," Johnny said, patting her shoulder. "Come on. Let's see what we can do."

He hurried back toward his black limousine with Elizabeth close behind. She followed him inside and was amazed to see a large control panel filled with strange-looking dials and levers.

"Sit down over there," the singer said, pointing to the white plush seat next to his. He sat in front of the control panel and began to push buttons and turn knobs. The chauffeur got into the back of the limousine while Johnny took command.

Outside, the crowd cheered one last salute to their hero. "Good luck," they called.

The limousine quivered, sang one golden note, then rose into the air. Elizabeth pressed her nose against the clear glass window and peered past the wings to the colorless sky. She saw the queen's gray ship still sailing through the air. Just inside the round window was Jessica, still held firmly in the wicked queen's grasp.

Elizabeth thought she could hear Jessica shouting.

"Hold on, Jessica. We're coming!" she called, hoping that her twin could hear.

"Hurry, Johnny," Elizabeth said, looking over her shoulder. "We've got to catch up with them."

Johnny moved a lever, then pushed a button. Elizabeth was pleased to feel their speed increase. "We're getting closer," she exclaimed. "Hang on, Jessica!"

Elizabeth could see her twin clearly now, struggling in the queen's grasp. Her own heart beat fast as she feared what would happen next to Jessica.

"How can we help her?" she asked Johnny. "Can you sing again?"

"I don't know if we're close enough," Johnny told her. His handsome face clouded with doubt as he tried to judge the distance. "I don't know if the magic will work from this far away."

"Please try," Elizabeth begged.

He pushed a button and the glass window on his side of the limousine slid down.

Johnny took a deep breath, and let his clear, strong voice ring out into the sky.

Elizabeth gazed at the pair on the other ship, almost afraid to watch.

As the pure notes of Johnny's song crossed the distance between them, the gray queen's face contorted with pain. She let go of the struggling girl to cover her ears. Jessica pulled away quickly and opened the door of the queen's ship.

"Here, Jessica!" Elizabeth called. She jumped up to stand on the edge of one of the neon-rimmed wings, holding out her hand toward her sister.

Johnny spoke to his magical limousine, and the black craft veered even closer to the queen's vessel.

"Jump," Elizabeth called. "I'll catch you!"

Jessica hesitated a moment, afraid of the open space between them.

"Jump," Elizabeth urged again. She stretched as far as she dared into the rushing wind. Determined to reach her sister, she hung on to the slender wing only by her fingertips.

Jessica seemed to gather all her courage. She took a great leap into the air.

Just when Elizabeth was sure she could grab her sister's hand and pull her safely into the flying car, a dark shape zoomed out of the sky.

"A witch!" Elizabeth gasped as a black-cloaked figure on a broomstick sped by.

The witch's gnarled face grinned in triumph as she snatched Jessica from Elizabeth's grasp.

Jessica shrieked as she was swept away on the back of the broomstick. Once again she had been kidnapped.

"Jessica!" Elizabeth called. Then she forgot her fear for her sister as she realized she was in danger. In her excitement she had leaned too far over the wing. Losing her hold, Elizabeth fell swiftly through the air.

Thirteen

◇

Down, down Elizabeth fell through the colorless sky. As she tumbled head over heels, she saw that the surface below was blue, with little white peaks that bobbed up and down. She was over an ocean! How would she survive such a fall?

There was no time to react. Moments later she hit the water with bone-jarring force. The impact thrust her deep beneath the waves. She struggled to get back to the surface but only sank deeper and deeper into the surprisingly clear blue water.

She wanted to sob, but she struggled to hold her breath, knowing she shouldn't inhale any of the briny water around her. A sudden movement in her T-shirt pocket made her look down. She was amazed to see the little mouse was still in her pocket. Her furry face had turned blue from holding her breath.

They continued to sink, until at last Elizabeth touched the sandy bottom of the ocean.

"Why are you making such a funny face?" a raspy voice asked.

Elizabeth whirled, gasping in spite of herself. She wasn't sure which surprised her more—that she wasn't drowning, or the bizarre sight of a large creature staring at her with long-lashed lavender eyes.

"I'm still alive!" she exclaimed in astonishment. She felt Allegra also relax. "How can I breathe under water?"

"This is the Enchanted Sea, silly," the creature told her. He unwound his long body and slid closer, as if to observe her better. "Didn't you know that?"

Elizabeth shook her head. "No, sir, I didn't." She examined the creature more closely. He had a long serpentine body covered with translucent scales that glowed with color. Scarlet, blue, violet, pink, gold—he looked like a rainbow. As the clear water bent the rays of sunlight sinking to the bottom of the ocean, the effect only enhanced his beauty.

His head was almost half the size of Elizabeth. Long and narrow, it resembled a sea horse. His lavender eyes were big and fringed with long lashes. His mouth was large, too, and filled with frighteningly sharp teeth. Elizabeth shivered.

Allegra glanced out of the top of Elizabeth's T-shirt pocket. She took one look at the creature's white fangs and darted back to the bottom of the pocket.

"Are you a—a sea serpent?" Elizabeth asked in a small voice.

"Well, of course," the creature replied, sounding surprised. "What did you think I was—a jellyfish?" He chuckled at his own joke.

"I've never seen a sea serpent before," Elizabeth hastened to explain. "You don't, uh, eat people, do you?"

The serpent looked offended. "Of course not. I'm almost a confirmed vegetarian. I only eat meat on Saturdays."

His big mouth widened into a smile that made Elizabeth fight back a shudder. Those teeth were so big and so pointed!

"And what day is it today?" Elizabeth asked.

"Ummm, Friday, I think." The serpent crossed its big eyes as it tried to count. "Do you think it's Friday?"

"Oh, I'm sure it's Friday," Elizabeth agreed. She made a silent vow to be long gone before Saturday rolled around.

"My name is Sidney," the creature told her.

"And mine is Elizabeth."

"How do you do, Elizabeth." Sidney dipped his long head to her.

Elizabeth couldn't offer to shake hands since the serpent didn't have any. She decided on a hasty curtsy instead. "How do you do," she answered politely.

"And what are you doing in the Enchanted Sea?" Sidney asked, focusing his lavender eyes on her.

Elizabeth realized that the serpent might not believe she'd come from a flying black limousine. "I fell out of a boat," she explained.

"What a shame," Sidney said, nodding his big head. "Actually, though, I'm glad."

"Why?" Elizabeth asked, her voice anxious. Was he already looking forward to Saturday?

"I get so bored down here," the serpent explained. "Do you know any games?"

"Uh, yes, I know lots of games," Elizabeth assured him, relieved that he wasn't thinking of his mealtime. "But I don't know what we can play on the bottom of the ocean."

Looking around the ocean floor, Elizabeth saw shapes in the shifting sand. She walked over to what looked like the outlines of a tower. Further on were the remains of walls and streets, nearly all covered with sand and seaweed.

"Was this once a city?" Elizabeth wondered.

"Of course," Sidney told her. "This is Atlantis, once the capital of a large island."

"What happened?"

"The island sank beneath the sea," the serpent explained. "And all the people left. But I like it; I like living in a palace."

Elizabeth looked at the crumbling ruins that the serpent regarded so fondly and tried not to giggle. She remembered what she was searching for. Bending over, she picked up a broken shell.

She began to draw a hopscotch grid in the sand but then stopped. That wouldn't do. The serpent didn't have any feet. And he was too big to play hide-and-seek. The nearest rocks were small, and the slender plants that grew from the sand, drifting back and forth in the water, would never disguise his bulk. Elizabeth certainly didn't want to play tag. Sidney might squash her by accident.

"Maybe we could play a board game," she said. "Oh, I know we can play chess." Elizabeth's nose wrinkled as she said, "No, we don't have any pieces."

"Pieces?" The serpent looked puzzled. "Should I tear something up?"

"No, no." Elizabeth shook her head, afraid of what he might decide to tear. "Oh dear, I can't think of anything."

A thin voice from her shirt pocket murmured, "Try checkers."

"That's it. Checkers."

She walked along the sandy bottom, collecting seashells and pebbles. When she had enough, she stooped down and scratched the outline of a checkerboard in the sand.

"You take the pebbles, and I'll take the seashells," she told Sidney. "Now watch. You jump your opponent's pieces like this."

She demonstrated the moves of the game, while Sidney watched with interest. *I just hope*, Elizabeth thought, *no one makes it to the other end of the board. How will I crown a seashell?*

The serpent took to the game with enthusiasm. When his turn came, he pushed the pebbles forward with his long nose. When he captured Elizabeth's seashells, he got so excited that he snorted in glee and scattered all the pieces.

Elizabeth patiently put them back into place,

and they finished the game. She managed to let the sea serpent win.

Sidney was ecstatic. "I won, I won," he chuckled. "I'm the champion. This is fun. I'm so glad you came, Elizabeth."

She nodded. "Now you must do me a favor," she told the big beast.

"What?" He lifted his long lashes and stared down at her.

"When I fell into the sea, I was chasing the Queen of Drudgery, who had stolen my sister. I almost grabbed her—my sister, I mean—when a witch with a long nose flew off with her. Do you know who that witch is, and where I might find her?"

The serpent raised his long nose, looking slightly alarmed. "That must be Grisolda. She's a cousin of the queen's. The queen must have used her own magic to summon her."

Elizabeth nodded. That made sense. "Where can I find Grisolda?"

Sidney shook his big head, rippling the water around them. "You don't want to do that! Grisolda's very powerful. She was banished by the wizard Merlin long ago and imprisoned in a seashell. When Atlantis sank, she escaped and took over Fairy Tale

Land. She made everyone so miserable with her wretched spells that it's now called Sorrowland. Merlin's away on his travels, and no one else is powerful enough to fight her. You certainly don't want to find her."

"I have to," Elizabeth told him. "I have to rescue my sister."

Sidney looked at her wistfully, his lavender eyes turning a dark purple. "Sisters must be wonderful things to make you risk Grisolda's wrath. I wish I had one."

"Sisters *are* special," Elizabeth agreed. "Now please tell me how to get to Sorrowland."

Sidney's long face assumed a stubborn look. "I won't," he said. "If you leave, I'll be lonely again. Who'll play checkers with me?"

"Sidney," Elizabeth said firmly, "you can't keep me here forever. If I'm unhappy, I can't play checkers anyway."

"You can't?"

"It's a rule of the game," Elizabeth assured him, crossing her fingers behind her back. "You must have another friend who wants to play with you. Surely there must be other creatures in the Enchanted Sea."

"There were, but they all left," Sidney sighed. "No one comes to see me anymore."

"Why not?" Elizabeth asked.

"Well," the serpent looked slightly guilty. "Saturdays, you know."

Elizabeth shook her head. "Sidney, you're going to have to forget about Saturdays. You can't expect to keep any friends if you go on eating them!"

"No?" The serpent frowned.

"Think about it," Elizabeth said.

He did. Finally he nodded slowly. "I suppose I could stick to seaweed," he suggested.

Elizabeth smiled at him. "I understand it's very nutritious."

"But it gets boring," Sidney complained.

"Do you want friends, or not?" Elizabeth asked. "With more players, you'd have lots of games to play."

"All right," Sidney agreed. "You're sure you can't stay?"

"No," Elizabeth told him. "Besides, if I stay, Grisolda might decide to come after me, too. You wouldn't want that."

"No, indeed," the serpent agreed, looking alarmed. "You'd better start right away."

"How do I get to Sorrowland?"

"Follow the Stream of Tears, all the way until the sunbeams disappear. When you reach the dark shore, you'll know you're there."

"Thank you, Sidney," Elizabeth told him. "Good luck with your checkers game, and your friends."

The big serpent swam along beside her to the top of a sandy knoll. He showed her the beginning of the path, then coiled his long body on the bottom of the sea and watched her go.

Elizabeth looked back for one last wave. She could have sworn the big serpent had tears in his lavender eyes.

"Wow," Allegra said, emerging at last from her pocket. "I was sure we were going to end up as appetizers. You were very brave, Elizabeth."

"I don't think he's really bad," Elizabeth said, defending the serpent. "He was just lonely."

She trudged along the sandy path. Walking against the force of the water was slow work. "This is going to take forever." Elizabeth sighed. "I wish I could move faster."

"Would you like a ride, Elizabeth?" someone asked.

Elizabeth gazed at what she'd assumed to be a

large, slightly rounded rock. A greenish head appeared, with large round eyes, then two pairs of flippers. It was a large green turtle.

"Hello," Elizabeth said in surprise. "How did you know my name?"

"I heard about your visit with Sidney," the turtle said. "News travels fast underwater, you know. If you've convinced Sidney to stop eating his neighbors, you've done all of us a big favor. Just hop on my back. I'll take you as far as you want to go."

"Thank you," Elizabeth said. "That would be a big help."

She climbed on top of the creature, gripping the edge of its wide shell. The turtle moved its big flippers and swam easily through the sea. Allegra put her head out of Elizabeth's pocket and watched as they floated through the water.

They swam through forests of coral, the branches sparkling with pink and lavender and orange. They saw waving tendrils of green and gray seaweed swaying gracefully with the current.

Elizabeth enjoyed watching the changing shape of the ocean floor. When the turtle slowed, she noticed that the light had gradually dimmed. Now she looked at the sandy bottom ahead of her. The water was dark and murky.

"Here we are," the turtle told them. "Are you sure you want to enter Sorrowland? Grisolda is very wicked and very powerful."

"I have to," Elizabeth said, climbing off the turtle's back. Her heart sank a little at the thought of her gloomy journey. "I have to find my sister."

"Good luck, then," the turtle said and headed back the way it had come.

Elizabeth straightened her shoulders and pushed ahead into the dark water. Almost at once the ocean floor began to slant upward. Elizabeth could hardly see, and she stumbled. Catching herself, she climbed slowly.

In a few minutes she saw a faint glimmer in front of her. Pushing onward, she emerged from the water. She took a deep breath and wiped the water out of her eyes, delighted to be back on land. But her smile faded when she saw what lay above the riverbed.

Fourteen

◇

What looked like a once-charming village lay before Elizabeth. Small stucco cottages with thatched roofs dotted the landscape. Some of the houses were trimmed in gay colors of blue, pink, and yellow.

The thatched roofs, though, were losing their straw. Each cottage needed a fresh coat of paint and the wooden trim was splintered and rotting. Cobwebs clung to the edges of the cracked and broken windows and dirt darkened the painted doors. The whole village wore an air of neglect and sadness.

"What could have happened here?" Elizabeth said to Allegra.

Then she remembered. This must have been the work of the evil Grisolda.

"Maybe we shouldn't have come," Allegra said, peering out from her pocket.

Elizabeth swallowed the lump in her throat.

They walked down the main street of the village. At first it seemed as if all the houses were deserted. Then she heard a noise coming from behind a small gray cottage. She walked cautiously around the house and peered into a paved courtyard.

A slender young woman dressed in rags knelt on the ground, scrubbing clothes in a wooden washtub. Sighing, she sat back on her heels and readjusted the checkered kerchief on her head.

"Who are you?" Elizabeth asked.

The young woman looked up, her expression sad and weary. "My name is Rapunzel. And who are you?" she asked.

Elizabeth couldn't believe this haggardly woman was the famous fairy-tale heroine. "I'm Elizabeth. I'm looking for my sister, who was kidnapped. But what are you doing here? I thought a prince rescued you from your tower and you lived happily ever after in his castle."

Rapunzel seemed ready to burst into tears. "That was true for a while," she admitted. "But look!" Rapunzel tore off her kerchief to reveal her head. It was completely bald.

Elizabeth stepped back in shock. She couldn't hide the surprised look on her face.

Rapunzel sighed sadly. "I know. It's ugly," she

said. "Grisolda did this. One day I woke up and all my beautiful golden hair was gone. One look at me and my prince was gone, too."

"That's terrible," Elizabeth exclaimed. "But surely he loved you for more than your hair."

"That's not all," Rapunzel said. "Look." She pointed to the delicate lines around her faded brown eyes. "See, wrinkles!" She held out her arms. "And liver spots, too. No wonder he didn't want me anymore."

Elizabeth didn't know whether to frown or laugh. "But Rapunzel," she argued. "That doesn't mean you're not still the same person. And anyway, everyone gets older."

"Not in fairy tales," Rapunzel replied. "Not normally. But Grisolda has stolen all our magic."

Elizabeth nodded. "Well, I guess so. But what kind of husband would throw you out because of that? He wasn't worth having if all he cared about was your beauty. You're really better off without him."

"He didn't act like that before Grisolda came," Rapunzel explained. "He was a truly wonderful person. But her magic affected everyone, and now we're all miserable!"

"I'm so sorry," Elizabeth said.

"You'd better not stay," Rapunzel warned. "She'll do something terrible to you, too."

Elizabeth felt a stab of fear, but she said in a determined voice, "I must find my sister and free her from the witch. There must be some way to defeat Grisolda!"

Rapunzel burst into tears. The large teardrops ran down the corner of her nose and dripped into her wash water. "I don't think you ever will," she said.

"Rapunzel!" A harsh voice called from inside the house.

"That's my mother," Rapunzel sobbed. "I'm living with her again." She sighed. "You'd better go."

Elizabeth nodded, still distressed. "Try not to worry," she said, turning back toward the pathway.

She continued along the street, looking for some sign of the wicked witch. A noise from another cottage made her pause. She approached the half-opened door cautiously and tiptoed up to look inside.

A beautiful young girl lay on a straw pallet. Tiny wisps of cloth barely covered her body. Her long blond hair stretched across her pillow and her pink lips let out a most horrific wail.

"My goodness," Elizabeth said, more loudly than she had intended. "So that's what that awful sound was."

Her words made the young woman start. She stopped crying and turned her blue eyes warily on Elizabeth. "Are you another witch?" she asked, frightened.

"No, no," Elizabeth assured her. "I'm just a girl, like you. What's your name?"

The girl got up and stood face-to-face with Elizabeth.

"I'm Thumbelina."

Elizabeth let out a gasp. "But—but you're so tall."

"Tell me about it," Thumbelina said, her voice choking with sobs. I was happy as a clam living with my prince in our shell until Grisolda came. Then she put a spell on me and turned me into this awful giant. I have no idea where my husband is now."

"Do you know where I can find Grisolda?" Elizabeth asked.

But Thumbelina didn't answer. She was too caught up in her own sorrow.

"Good-bye," Elizabeth said. She tiptoed away as the heartbroken princess cried herself to sleep.

"I didn't know anyone could cry so loudly," Elizabeth told Allegra as they walked back up the street.

"That's probably part of Grisolda's spell," the mouse said wisely.

Elizabeth glanced into the next house and saw a tall young man bent over a desk, writing with a quill pen. He was dressed in a green three-piece suit and looked familiar to Elizabeth.

"Do you know where Grisolda is?" Elizabeth asked.

The man looked up, a sad expression on his face. He shook his head. "You don't want to find Grisolda," he told her, standing and stretching his tired muscles. "I avoid her as much as possible."

Elizabeth looked up at his tall form and gasped. "Aren't you Peter Pan?"

He nodded sadly.

"But you've grown up!"

"I know. I'm six-two and still growing," he confirmed. "It's a great disappointment. I never wanted to grow up. I wanted to fight pirates and hunt Indians and live in a tree. Grisolda changed all that."

"You poor thing," Elizabeth sympathized. "What are you doing here?"

"I'm an accountant," Peter said with a sigh, sitting back down to his work.

Elizabeth couldn't bear his sad expression. She hurried back to the street.

She continued until she came to a large house surrounded by an overgrown garden. The once-white picket fence was broken down and covered with peeling paint. Elizabeth could hear voices behind the house. She opened the gate, and she and Allegra walked up the gravel path.

A small white rabbit dressed in a pink pinafore scampered past, followed by two small kittens in striped jerseys. "Come back with our ball," they shrieked as they ran.

"What naughty children!" Elizabeth said to Allegra. "Whose house is this?" She was about to knock on the door when a figure came out of the house. It was a large white rabbit wearing a striped vest with a watch chain looped over one pocket. He carried a handful of small sweaters and knit hats and looked very distracted.

"Oh dear, oh dear," he muttered. "The children have gone out without their sweaters again. No pie for them tonight—again. Oh dear, oh dear."

"Pardon me," Elizabeth said. "Do you know where I can find Grisolda?"

The rabbit shuddered. "Don't mention that name."

"But I need to find her," Elizabeth told him.

The white rabbit pulled out his watch, dropping a sweater or two in the process, and shook his head. "I was supposed to have tea with Alice this afternoon, and now I'll never make it. Oh dear, oh dear."

Collecting his sweaters, he hurried off after his errant children. Elizabeth was tempted to follow him and see how he managed to put knit hats on little kittens with long ears, but she decided she had better move on.

Elizabeth and Allegra continued down the street. They soon left the little village behind. The next house they came to was very large. Elizabeth approached it cautiously and peered through a large side window. When she saw it was empty, she walked inside and found a collection of strange wooden furniture. The big chairs all had ferocious faces carved into their backs. They were so large that when Elizabeth climbed into one for just a moment to rest her tired legs, she couldn't even reach the floor.

She put her feet onto a padded stool.

"Ouch," a voice said.

Elizabeth drew her feet back in alarm. Looking closer, she saw that this footstool not only had a face at one side, but it talked!

"You didn't have to step so hard," the footstool complained.

"I'm sorry," Elizabeth said. "I didn't know—I mean, who are you?"

"I used to be Hansel," the stool said with a sigh. "My sister Gretel is over there." His eyes looked in the direction of an arm chair on the other side of the room. "We made Grisolda angry and she turned us into furniture."

"What did you do?" Elizabeth asked.

"We ate some of her gingerbread house. Maybe it wasn't such a smart thing to do, but we were very hungry—and that other witch hadn't minded when we ate her house."

"I thought she almost ate you," Elizabeth pointed out.

"Well, that's true," Hansel admitted. "But it all worked out in the end. Not like now. Grisolda didn't have to make me into a footstool."

"That's true," Elizabeth agreed. "Do you know where I can find her?"

"She lives in the gingerbread house just past the first windmill," Hansel told her. "But please don't make her angry. If she finds out I ratted she'll turn me into firewood and put me in her furnace!"

The little stool shuddered, making a knocking sound on the hard stone floor.

"I won't tell," Elizabeth said quickly. "I've got to go now."

"Yes," Hansel agreed. "You'd better. The giant who lives here will be home soon for dinner."

Elizabeth and Allegra wasted no time getting out of the big house. Once they were safely out of sight of the giant's house, they came to a crossroads.

Elizabeth asked, "Do you see the windmill?"

Allegra ran up Elizabeth's long blond hair and stood on top of her head, scanning the horizon. "That way," she pointed.

Elizabeth sped in the direction Allegra had pointed. Soon the path narrowed. A straggling bunch of thornbushes blocked the way. Elizabeth pushed through the prickly plants, scratching her ankles and arms as she did. Beyond them she could see the eaves of a cottage.

"It's the gingerbread house! The evil witch's house!"

Fifteen

◇

Elizabeth, with Allegra in her pocket, crept closer to Grisolda's house. The walls were made of sturdy gingerbread. Gumdrops and candy canes formed the doorframe, and licorice sticks and lollipops framed the windows. All that candy made Elizabeth remember that it had been ages since she'd eaten. She was tempted to break off a tiny bit of gingerbread, but remembering Hansel's story, she decided against it.

"Be quiet," Allegra warned nervously, "or she'll hear us."

Elizabeth tiptoed up to the window and peeked inside. At first all she could see were four very dusty chairs and a wooden table. An old-fashioned wardrobe sat in one corner, and a rusty iron stove in the other. There was no sign of the witch or Jessica.

"Where can they be?" Elizabeth murmured to Allegra. The little mouse shook her head.

"I don't know. I guess we'll have to look inside."

Taking a deep breath, Elizabeth pushed open the front door. The cottage seemed larger on the inside than it had from the window, and there was no one in sight.

A scrawny plant bearing one large orange flower rested on the window ledge behind a wooden chest. Elizabeth lifted the lid of the chest to peek inside. A collection of black capes and pointed hats made her shiver. She lowered the wooden lid carefully so it wouldn't make a noise. As she did, she brushed the leaves of the odd-looking plant. To her amazement, the orange flower opened its petals. Inside was a row of small, sharp teeth that snapped eagerly at her fingers.

Elizabeth pulled her hand away quickly, shuddering at the near miss. "You're not munching on me," she told the flower crossly.

"Witches' posy," Allegra said. "I've heard of that flower."

"Now you tell me!" Elizabeth scolded. "I still don't see any sign of my sister."

She tiptoed across the stone floor and peeked

inside a wooden cupboard, but all she found was a collection of cracked dishes. No sister.

"Ugh," Elizabeth said. When she shut the door again, the dust from the cupboard shelves blew up into her face and she sneezed loudly.

"Hush," Allegra warned from her pocket. "Witches have very keen ears."

Elizabeth rubbed her nose. "I couldn't help it," she told the mouse. "Where can Jessica be?"

When she spoke her twin's name, a sudden knocking from the stove made Elizabeth jump. "What's that?" She tiptoed across the stone floor and approached the rusty old stove with caution. "Is someone there?"

The knocking became even louder. Elizabeth, fearing some magical trick, held her breath as she touched the oven door. With one swift motion she pulled it open.

Out tumbled Jessica, all in a heap!

"Jessica!" Elizabeth cried. She ran forward to hug her sister.

"It's about time!" Jessica said, rubbing her elbow, which had been bruised by the hard floor.

"I've been looking for you for ages," Elizabeth told her. "Are you all right?"

Jessica nodded. Her face was streaked with dirt, and her green jumpsuit had a hole in the right knee. But she was the same sister that Elizabeth had last seen flying away on Grisolda's broomstick.

"Why were you in the oven?" Elizabeth asked. An awful thought occurred to her. "Don't tell me the witch was going to cook you for dinner?"

"She did think about it," Jessica said matter-of-factly. "Fortunately, the oven was broken. So she ordered pizza instead."

"You poor thing," Elizabeth exclaimed.

"I know, I was upset, too." Jessica nodded sadly. "It was a Deluxe, with everything on it. I could smell the pepperoni so strongly I could almost taste it and the wicked witch didn't even offer me a piece."

"Let's get out of here," Elizabeth suggested. "Then we'll both get something to eat."

"Let me just take a piece of the window frame," Jessica begged. "I'm really starving."

"I don't think you should, Jessica," Elizabeth warned. But it was too late. Jessica had already broken a piece of gingerbread from the side of the window and was munching it.

A moment later, the whole house shuddered. "We'd better get out of here," Jessica said.

Again they were too late. The door of the wooden wardrobe swung open, and a wrinkled face with a long nose and dark evil eyes appeared.

As the black-robed witch stepped through the opening, Elizabeth could see that the wardrobe covered an entrance to a set of steps that led down into the darkness.

The witch straightened herself to her full height as a sleek black cat jumped through the doorway and curled up at her mistress's feet.

Inside Elizabeth's pocket, Allegra shivered and ducked out of sight.

The witch eyed the two girls, stretching her purple lips into a ghastly smile. "And who is this? Someone raiding my larder?"

Elizabeth gulped. Beside her, she felt Jessica tremble. Elizabeth put one arm around Jessica and faced the witch squarely.

"You have no right to kidnap people, much less cook them for dinner!" she cried. "I only came here to rescue my sister."

"And who said you could tear my poor cottage into bits?" The witch frowned.

Elizabeth shook her head. "That's what you get for starving your prisoners," she declared. "It was only a tiny piece. Please let us go. We won't bother anything else. Jessica is my twin sister; we have to be together."

The witch began to cackle. "So you want to be together, do you? Indeed, you two do look like a mirror image. So you shall be—*together!*"

She muttered a few words, then waved her hand through the air, leaving a trail of sparks. Elizabeth shook her head, trying to clear her vision. She heard Jessica shriek, and something tugged at her side.

Allegra had been peering over the edge of her pocket. Shaken by the sharp motion, she lost her grip and fell to the floor. Fortunately no one noticed her. The little mouse ran to hide behind a chair leg.

"Ouch!" Elizabeth exclaimed. "What are you doing?"

She turned to see why her twin was tugging so painfully at her. Her mouth fell open.

"We're stuck together," Jessica wailed. "This is terrible!"

Indeed they seemed to be melded together at hand and foot. The result was that when one moved, the other did, too.

"What are we going to do?" Jessica demanded, trying to move forward. But her right foot couldn't move without Elizabeth's left foot going with it.

Elizabeth was almost jerked off her own feet. She tried to walk forward, too, but only managed to swing into her sister. They bumped heads with a painful thump.

"Ow-w!" Jessica yelled. "What have you done to us, you old biddy!"

The witch continued to cackle. "You said you wanted to be together."

"Lizzie, this is your fault," Jessica complained. She tried to push her blond hair out of her eyes. But Elizabeth's hand came up, too, and accidentally poked her in the eye.

"Ow-w," Jessica moaned.

"I'm sorry. I didn't mean to hit you." Elizabeth frowned at the witch. "This wasn't what I meant at all. There's such a thing as too much togetherness!"

"It's too late to think of that," Jessica snapped. "Look at the shape we're in. We can't even walk."

"Look, I think if we move together, we can do it," Elizabeth suggested. They tried to take a step in unison, but only managed to go in a circle. They ended up back where they had started.

"Now what?" Elizabeth said. She eyed her twin doubtfully.

"This is worse than the oven," Jessica said, her tone impatient.

"Fine! Next time I'll just leave you to the witch. Who cares if you end up as the main course? After the way you broke your promise—" Elizabeth stopped and bit her lip. She hadn't come through all these adventures just to quarrel with her sister.

Jessica held back her next complaint, too, and the two of them stared at each other.

"You did come after me," Jessica said. "Not everyone would have done that."

"I would," Elizabeth said, a tiny smile replacing her frown.

Jessica nodded. "I'm glad you're my sister," she said. "And I'm sorry I left you and sat with Lila."

"Maybe I expected too much of you," Elizabeth said. "You have your own friends. Just because you're my twin doesn't mean you can't make plans of your own."

"But no one else means as much to me as you do, Lizzie," Jessica said. The two sisters exchanged a quick, one-handed hug, trying not to get totally entangled.

The witch's laughter faded as the two sisters made up. She frowned at them. "I'll just have to think of something else," she muttered. "Maybe I'll turn you and all the people in the village into frogs. What a nice chorus that would make. Now let me think of a good spell," she cackled.

The twins clutched each other. Then the witch's black cat began to sniff the air, its long whiskers quivering with excitement. It crept forward, its body crouched low to the floor, straight toward the chair leg which hid Allegra from view.

"Look out, Allegra," Elizabeth cried.

The little mouse saw her enemy approaching and scrambled wildly to get out of danger. She ran toward the safety of Elizabeth's pocket. But, confused by the identical twins, she turned toward Jessica instead. The little animal ran up inside Jessica's pants leg and crouched behind her knee.

"Oh," Jessica said, surprised. The mouse's tiny feet tickled as they clung to her leg, and she began to giggle.

"What's this?" the witch exclaimed. "How dare you laugh at me? I'll turn you into a turnip!"

Despite this threat, Jessica couldn't stop. She laughed even harder. The witch's green face began to darken. "Stop!" she commanded.

Elizabeth knew she should have been frightened, but she found her twin's laughter contagious. She, too, began to giggle.

"Stop," the witch commanded. But her voice sounded feeble. She began to shake.

''What's happening?" Jessica said.

Elizabeth's laughter also died as she stared at the witch.

But the witch had recovered. Her shaking stopped and she glared at the girls.

"Just for that, I'm going to think of the worst spell I've ever conjured!" she shrieked. "You'll moan and groan until you're old and gray!"

"What did we do?" Jessica asked, staring at her twin in confusion. "What's she angry about now?"

"I think I know," Elizabeth said. "Laugh!"

"At what?" Jessica looked bewildered.

There wasn't time to explain. Already the witch had begun to mutter, casting dark looks at the girls. Elizabeth tickled her sister.

"Stop it," Jessica yelled. But she began to giggle. "Take that," she said, poking her twin in the ribs.

Elizabeth laughed, too. She was pleased to see Grisolda stop in the middle of her spell and begin to shake.

"Don't stop laughing," Elizabeth said, gasping. Her sides ached, but she laughed anyhow.

Jessica continued to giggle.

The witch shook harder. She rocked back and

forth until, before the girls' astonished eyes, she began to crack. Like a shattered glass, the cracks spread until the witch dropped into a thousand splintered pieces.

The twins were silent. "What happened?" Jessica asked.

"The laughter destroyed her," Elizabeth said. "That's why the witch kept everyone here so miserable. She didn't dare allow anyone to laugh."

Elizabeth stepped closer to view the remains of the witch. She looked like a jigsaw puzzle. The black cat jumped through the open window, disappearing into the bushes.

"Hooray!" Jessica exclaimed. "We're free!"

Sure enough, Elizabeth looked down and found that she and her twin were once more separate people.

They hugged each other again.

Allegra dropped back to the stone floor now that the cat had gone.

"You did it," she cried. "You destroyed Grisolda! How thankful the villagers will be."

The three of them walked out of the gingerbread house. The thornbushes had disappeared, replaced by flowering pink roses. Allegra and the twins followed the path easily toward the fairyland village. At the crossroads they met a crowd coming to see what had broken Grisolda's spells.

"Elizabeth?" the white rabbit called, "what did you do to the witch?"

"We laughed at her," Elizabeth explained. "She couldn't stand the sound of true laughter. It destroyed her."

"Hurrah!" the villagers shouted, laughing themselves.

"Rapunzel," Elizabeth said, hardly believing her eyes. The lovely young princess walked up the path, her beautiful golden hair flowing behind her. "Is it really you?"

The princess nodded, smiling sweetly. "Yes, my hair is back and so is my prince. Isn't it wonderful? I'm going to meet him at the castle right now."

"And look at me." Elizabeth turned around, trying to find the source of that voice. "Down here."

Right at Elizabeth's feet stood Thumbelina, once more as tiny as a blade of grass. "Now my prince will recognize me. We can be together again."

While Jessica stared at the fairy-tale characters, Elizabeth turned to a young boy, whose three-piece suit hung on him like a tent.

"Peter?" she guessed.

"It's me." The boy grinned. "I left my accounting books. I'm going back to the woods to find the Lost Boys. Thanks, Elizabeth!"

"Thanks," Hansel added, waving his arms to show Elizabeth he was no longer a giant's footstool.

"Thank you," the rest of the villagers chorused. "We'll never forget you, Elizabeth."

"I'm so glad you're all free," Elizabeth told them. "And I've found my sister at last. But now how do we get back home?"

"That's easy," Rapunzel told them. "Now that Grisolda is gone, our magic has been restored. We'll put you in a magic boat and send you home."

They all walked down to the river where a little red boat awaited them.

Allegra shook hands with both girls. "I'm going to stay in Fairy Tale Land," she told them. "This is my home."

Elizabeth bent over to shake the little mouse's hand. "It was great to have you along. Thanks for your help, Allegra."

Elizabeth and Jessica stepped into the boat, sitting together this time. Hansel pushed them away from the dock.

"How do we steer it?" Elizabeth called.

"You don't have to do a thing," Allegra cried out. "The boat knows the way. *Bon voyage!*"

The boat began to float down the river. The people of Fairy Tale Land waved good-bye, then faded out of sight as the boat picked up speed.

"It'll be good to get back to our own world," Elizabeth told her sister. "Adventures are fun, but they can be scary, too."

Jessica nodded. Then she gulped.

"What's wrong?" Elizabeth asked. She looked up and saw that the green fields beside the river had given way to steep cliffs. The river had narrowed, and the current pushed their little boat faster and faster toward a towering wall of stone.

"We're going to crash!" Jessica wailed.

Elizabeth saw that the boat was heading toward a dark tunnel. Would they make it through the narrow opening?

"Hang on to me," she yelled, not wanting to lose her sister again. Clinging together, the two girls were swept into the darkness.

Sixteen

◇

Elizabeth shut her eyes as the darkness engulfed her. When she saw a glimmer of light through her eyelids, she opened them, ready to laugh with Jessica at their unnecessary fears. But to her surprise, she saw that Jessica was crying!

"What's wrong?" Elizabeth mumbled.

"She's coming around," someone said.

Elizabeth blinked, confused. Why was Jessica standing over her, instead of seated beside her in the magic boat? And why was Elizabeth no longer in the boat, but stretched out on a dock?

Turning her head, Elizabeth recognized a whole crowd of her friends. Amy, Julie, Brooke, and several other classmates watched her anxiously.

"Oh, Lizzie," Jessica sobbed. "I thought you were dead! I'm sorry I was so thoughtless this morning. Please forgive me."

"But you already apologized," Elizabeth murmured.

A figure in a white-ruffled shirt and black tights bent over her. Elizabeth gasped. Prince Kendrick?

But this young man looked concerned. "Does your head hurt?" he asked.

"My head?" Elizabeth discovered that her head was throbbing. She touched it gingerly. "What happened?"

"Don't you remember?" Amy spoke quickly, her tone anxious. "We bumped heads at the end of the castle ride. You blacked out. We were all so worried about you!"

"What?" Elizabeth looked around. She saw that she was lying on the dock at the entrance to King Abelard's Castle. Then all her adventures—with the knights, Johnny Buck, Allegra, the witch—had they all been only a dream?

"But Rapunzel and Hansel—" she murmured. It had seemed so real. How could she have dreamed it all?

"We haven't gotten to those rides yet," Amy told her. "But we will."

Elizabeth nodded. "Now that the witch is destroyed, it'll be fun again," she said.

Jessica looked frightened. "Lizzie, what are you talking about?"

Elizabeth tried to pull her thoughts back to the real world. "I'm fine, Jess. Don't worry."

"Let me take you to the first-aid station," the young attendant offered. "A registered nurse is on duty."

Elizabeth shook her head. "I'm all right, really. Thank you anyhow."

Jessica added, "Don't worry. I'm going to stay right by her side the whole day! I'll look after her."

Elizabeth grinned. "Remember, there's such a thing as too much togetherness," she told her twin.

Jessica looked confused. "What?"

"Never mind," Elizabeth said. She stood up. Her knees were weak, and her head ached slightly, but she wasn't really hurt.

"Come on," she said to her friends. "Let's not waste any more time. The Enchanted Forest awaits us!"

Laughing, the girls hurried to catch the next ride. They walked through Hansel and Gretel's Woods, admiring the colorful gingerbread house and peered into shop windows on the plaza.

After they left the plaza, Elizabeth reached into

her pocket, pulled out her camera, and checked the exposure indicator. It was still set at one. "Hey, Amy, would you mind taking a picture of me and Jessica?"

"Not at all," Amy said.

As Elizabeth posed with her sister, she looked around the park with delight. All the buildings sparkled with new paint. The flower beds were crowded with colorful blossoms.

"I just love the Enchanted Forest," she said with a sigh.

It turned out to be a wonderful day. The Sweet Valley kids went on all their old favorite rides as well as the new ones. When they came to the Adventures Under the Sea in 3-D, Jessica was thrilled that the frames of the viewing glasses were purple, her favorite color. Elizabeth smiled as the rest of the girls shrieked over the sea creatures, remembering the adventure she had shared with Sidney the sea serpent. How could she have imagined such a thing? She giggled to herself, marveling at her own imagination.

The rest of Fairy Tale Land was simply wonderful. Elizabeth and Jessica rode the brightly colored horses on the old carousel, then whirled around the Witch's Magic Cauldrons, feeling dizzy but incredibly happy to be together. Elizabeth even agreed to go through Caterpillar Cavern, even though she'd already been through it once . . . in her mind.

It was lunchtime, but Elizabeth was too excited to eat. "Let's head for the Fun Zone," she told Jessica. "I understand there's a terrific new ride."

"The Super Coaster?" Jessica asked incredulously. "You really want to go on it with me?"

"Sure," Elizabeth said. "I'd do anything for my sister." She linked her arm in Jessica's. After all the adventures she'd just been through, a little old roller coaster didn't seem scary at all.

Still, Elizabeth closed her eyes as they reached the top of the first drop. It wasn't so bad, she realized, when she couldn't see where she was going. She joined Jessica in delighted screams as they twisted and turned around the giant ride. But unlike Jessica, she didn't wave her arms in the air when they soared down the steep inclines. She wasn't *that* brave.

It was just about six o'clock when the girls finally trailed back down the main plaza. Tired but happy, they stopped at one of the gift shops and picked up some souvenirs of their trip. Elizabeth bought a lavender sea serpent puppet.

As the small group of girls hurried across the

plaza, past the Farmer in the Dell, one of the life-sized animals waved at them.

"Look, you guys," Amy said. "The white mouse moved."

Jessica had walked ahead and didn't hear. Elizabeth turned quickly, smiling at the costumed animal.

"'Bye, Elizabeth," she called.

Elizabeth did a double take, then decided her imagination must be working overtime.

But Amy had heard, too.

"The mouse talked!" she exclaimed in surprise. "These characters *never* talk. And how on earth did she know your name?"

Elizabeth shrugged and smiled, then waved at Allegra one last time before slipping past the gates to the waiting bus.

SPECIAL FREE OFFER

Bring Sweet Valley Home!

Be a part of Sweet Valley by starting your own "I Love Sweet Valley" Group! Just fill out the coupon below and you'll receive FREE everything you'll ever need or want to share Sweet Valley with your friends!

- ID cards
- Bookmarks
- Stickers
- SWEET VALLEY® Memo Pads
- 4-color Poster

FILL IN THE COUPON BELOW AND MAIL.

"I Love Sweet Valley" Kit, PO Box 1004, South Holland, IL 60473

Please send me the *free* Sweet Valley items to start my own "I Love Sweet Valley" Group.

Name _____

Address _____

City/State _____ Zip _____

Offer expires and completed coupon must be received by December 31, 1988 and is *only* good while supplies last. Allow 6–8 weeks for delivery.

SVC 2—6/88

IT ALL STARTED WITH

THE

SWEET VALLEY TWINS

For two years teenagers across the U.S. have been reading about Jessica and Elizabeth Wakefield and their High School friends in SWEET VALLEY HIGH books. Now in books created especially for you, author Francine Pascal introduces you to Jessica and Elizabeth when they were 12, facing the same problems with their folks and friends that you do.

Special Offer
Buy a Bantam Book
for only 50¢.

Now you can order the exciting books you've
been wanting to read straight from Bantam's
latest catalog of hundreds of titles. *And* this
special offer gives you the opportunity to purchase
a Bantam book for only 50¢. Here's how:

By ordering any five books at the regular
price per order, you can also choose any other
single book listed (up to a $5.95 value) for only
50¢. Some restrictions do apply, so for further
details send for Bantam's catalog of titles today.

Just send us your name and address and
we'll send you Bantam Book's SHOP AT
HOME CATALOG!